Belle Publishing LLC
1200 S Air Depot Blvd
Suite G
Midwest City, OK 73110
www.bellepublishingllc.co
bellepublishingllc@gmail.com

First Edition
ISBN- 978-1-953928-43-6

Killa City III
The Final Chapter

By Anthony KinFolks Strickland

Killa City III
The Final Chapter

Chapter 1

Faba looked at Pain then back at her.

"Aight." Faba said while dialing a number.

"Yeah." Nick said when he answered. "What's up?"

"Your people got Yetta." Faba said. "Where the fuck they going?"

"Them bitch ass niggas went against my word!" Nick screamed through the phone. "Mutha fuckas!"

Nick hung up the phone and dialed Smooth but didn't get an answer. He took a chance and called Yetta's phone.

"Seriously?" Big Ben said when he answered. "Why the fuck are you calling this phone?"

"Nigga I told you not to make that dumb ass move!" Nick yelled. "That's why you will forever be a corner boy."

"Dumb huh?" Big Ben said. "Them bitches either gonna pay up or I'm gone kill all three of these bitches one by one."

"Three?!" Nick screamed. "I know your dumb ass don't think the King of *KILLA CITY* gonna pay you and let you live after taking his daughter on the day of Bam's funeral? You got to be the stupidest nigga alive."

"Naw Nick we untouchable." Big Ben concluded as he hung up.

Nick looked at the phone to see how long they were on the call before he dialed Wallace's number.

"Rayford Bail Bonds." Wallace said when he answered.

"Yo, I need a trace." Nick said. "I'm gonna text you the number."

"Aight Boss." Wallace said opening his computer, "How soon do you need this info?"

"ASAP!" Nick replied as he hung up. He texted Wallace then went to change clothes before he grabbed his keys and left the room.

"I can't believe this hoe ass nigga put his hands on my girl." Nick mumbled. "I gotta get her back." He hit the garage button and put the car in drive ready to pull off until he seen people standing in front of his car.

"What the fuck?" Nick yelled before he heard the CLICK CLACK from a gun that one of the men were holding.

"Get the fuck out the car!" Doe said as he and Gripp came into the light. "Stand up for the King."

"FUCK." Nick said opening the door. He stepped out the car and shut the door behind him before turning towards Gripp.

"Naw playboy." Doe said still pointing his gun, "Lay that shit on the hood."

Nick watched him hard as he pulled out his 45 and laid it on the hood before he looked back at Gripp.

"So, what?" Nick said. "You came all the way here to kill me?"

"As much as I would like to put your head through that windshield." Gripp said, pulling out a cigar. "It's not your time to die."

"Then what the fuck you want?" Nick said.

Doe walked up on Nick and raised his arm before Gripp spoke.

"Naw, Doe." Gripp said looking at Nick. "Now, where the fuck is my daughter and I'm only gonna ask once."

"So, you niggas roll up on me thinking I got a death wish or mentally retarded?" Nick said laughing.

"Nigga, to be honest I don't give a fuck what you think." Doe said putting his gun on the hood. "Fuck you."

"Nigga please." Nick said turning back to Gripp. "I will deal with you in a minute."

Gripp stood with a cold look in his eyes as he waited for Nick to continue.

"Number one, I have always loved Yetta so I would never put her in harm's way. And two, I wouldn't be stupid enough to lay a pinky on your daughter let alone kidnap her. I just found out myself." Nick said

Gripp lit his cigar as he stared into Nick's eyes. He puffed it a few times before he spoke again.

"So, you say you just found out?" Gripp said. "But your people are behind it right?"

"Yeah." Nick said as he pulled out a Newport. "The bitch ass niggas just answered Yetta's phone."

"So, why shouldn't I just let Doe put a bullet in your head right now like this bullshit didn't start with you?" Gripp said with a soft voice.

Nick lit his cigarette before he spoke.

"Honestly I don't give a fuck what you do Gripp cause I ain't scared of dying and I for damn sho ain't scared of this nigga here." He said pointing at Doe. "All I ask is that you wait so I can put a bullet in Big Ben's head first."

"This nigga got balls!" Doe said walking up to Nick. "Big ones I tell ya but nigga I'll beat your ass."

Nick's phone started ringing in the car, so he stepped back and gave Gripp a nod before looking to see it was Wallace calling.

"Aye!" Nick said looking back at Doe. "I need to answer that call so don't be trying to sneak me when I turn the fuck around."

"Trust me," Doe said grabbing the gun off the hood, "We gonna catch a real fair one cause I don't want you to have no excuses about why I beat your ass."

Gripp laughed as Nick reached in and grabbed the phone. He answered and put the phone on speaker.

"What up my guy?" Nick said setting the phone on the hood. "Tell me you got something."

"I got a few somethings for you bro." Wallace said clearing his throat. "But man, you gonna owe me for this one."

"Well damn." Nick said. "You must have some good shit to tell me."

"This information is worth every penny my friend." Wallace said laughing. "You know how I do."

"Yeah, I do." Nick said, "So, what's up?"

"I tracked the location of that number you gave me to Houston Texas." Wallace said.

"Texas?" Nick started, "What the fuck them bitches got up they sleeve?"

"I don't know but the phone is still moving." Wallace said.

"Keep me up on every stop made." Nick said looking at Gripp. "I mean every stop."

"I'll do you one better." Wallace said hitting the keyboard. "We hacked the phone and put a tracking app on it. Long as it is on, you got your location."

"That's why you my nigga bro." Nick said laughing.

"Go get your girl. Bro." Wallace said. "I will send you the link and let me know if you need anything else."

"Already." Nick said picking up his phone. "Gone."

"Gone." Wallace said as they hung up.

Gripp and Doe turned and started walking to the car when Doe turned and seen Nick still standing by his car.

"Mane, bring your bitch ass on!" Doe yelled as he opened the truck door.

Nick walked to the truck and got in the backseat.

"Keep it up and I'm gonna slap the Arkansas in you lil boy." Nick said closing the door.

"Fuck you, Cuz." Doe said as he put the truck in drive.

Nick's phone went off as they left the driveway. He looked at the message and clicked the link. The web pulled up a location on the south side of Houston.

"Looks like they on the Southside, here's the address." Nick said showing the phone to Doe.

"Aight." Doe said putting the address in the GPS, "Time to make that call boss man."

Gripp looked at Doe before picking up his phone. He took a deep breath before he dialed the number. Puffing his Cigar, he put the phone to his ear.

Ma Williams and Faba were still sitting in the car when the phone rang. Faba looked at the screen to see who was calling.

"Aye, Ma." Faba said handing her the phone. "It's King Gripp."

Ma Williams took the phone. She answered it with a very soft tone.

"Hello King." She spoke. "Where are you?"

"I'm in Arkansas, Ma Williams." He said as he lit his cigar again." About to head to Houston."

"Arkansas?!" She said surprised. "What's going on there?"

"Soon as they got took, me and Doe took a helicopter to Arkansas and ran up on Nick." Gripp said. "Now, we headed to Houston."

He hit his cigar before he continued.

"Long story short Nick didn't know about the shit until you called. He got his people to put a tracker on Yetta's phone and right now it's in Houston so that's where we going."

"We?" She questioned. "So, you didn't kill Nick?"

"No ma'am." Gripp said laughing. "I didn't."

"Good." She said laughing with him, "Also there's something else."

"What's that?" Gripp asked.

"Cain called as well." She replied. "Said he heard about the girls, and we better handle it before he does."

"Ma Williams." Gripp said taking a deep breath, "I have told you before I'm not worried about him or anyone else talking this partnership shit. I don't need him to find what's mine, I got it."

"That much I know." She said with a smile. "I will call everyone. See you soon."

"Indeed." Gripp said. "And tell Faba I promise to save one of these niggas for him to kill."

"Indeed." Faba said laughing hard in the background. "Appreciate that bro!"

"Talk to you later." She said hanging up the phone.

Gripp hung up the phone and laughed then sat back rolling down the window.

"What's so funny?" Doe asked.

"She thought I killed Nick." He said laughing, she knows me so well."

"Haha!" Doe said loudly. "Hell yeah, she do. Let's go get these niggas."

He got on the highway as Nick lit a blunt then handed it to him before lighting his own. Doe took the blunt and looked at Nick.

"Appreciate it." Doe said. "I'm still gone beat your ass though."

"Doe hit the blunt hard then started smacking his lips. He looked at Gripp before he turned towards Nick.

"I see you got some good taste, Doe said as he hit it again, this some straight gas."

"I know nigga, Nick said as he hit his blunt, enjoy nigga."

"Oh, I will asshole," Doe said turning up the music

They all sat back and enjoyed as the ice cream cake hit their systems. The high made the ride feel like a flight.

"Like I told you earlier," Nick said. "When this is over, we can catch a fair one and I got fifty stacks that these hands knock your ass out bruh!"

"Fifty racks?!" Gripp said laughing. "That nigga serious den a mutha fucker but can your ass even fight?"

Gripp turned to look at Nick as Doe turned down the music.

"If this nigga takes this bet, I guess we gonna find out." Nick said hitting the blunt slowly. "So, what's up Doe?"

"Bitch ass nigga you know I'm taking that shit." Doe said laughing hard. "My car needs some new rims anyway."

They all started laughing as Gripp turned up the music then sat back as they rode the highway headed to Houston.

Ma Williams gave the phone back to Faba then looked at him and smiled.

"Well, it looks like the King has a new soldier." She said laughing. "He allowed Nick to live and that is such a surprise to me."

"Shit not me." Faba said shaking his head. "Not a fucking surprise at all."

"Why you say that?" She asked, while sitting down "You know something I don't?"

"Ma, Gripp don't know about them college days." Faba started. "Because Yetta didn't tell anyone about that shit except me and Kesha plus the little bit you know."

"Tell me you're joking." She said in shock. "That may turn into a problem if he finds out."

"A big one." Faba said. "But right now, it's not our problem."

"You're right about that." She said getting up. "Let's go ahead and get to this hospital before they start wondering where we are."

"Yes ma'am." He stood with her. "I'll meet you in the front garage."

He walked out as she grabbed her purse, gun and keys then headed out the door as well. Once she made it to the garage, Faba was standing by the car holding the door when she walked over to the car. After she got in, he closed the door then got in on the other side.

They both sat back as Alex drove off headed to the hospital. She cracked the window then took a deep breath as she closed her eyes and enjoyed the outside air and a moment of peace.

Chapter 2

Smooth pulled into the gas station as they made it to Houston. Everyone got out the car as the van pulled in behind them.

"So, what's your fucking plan?" Smooth said to Big Ben as he got out the van. "Or are you just making one as we go?"

"Why you ask so many fucking questions about shit that ain't your fucking business?" Big Ben said pushing pass him. "Now get the fuck out my way."

"Hold the fuck up you bitch ass nigga." Smooth said grabbing his shoulder. "Your gay ass already lied to me once and that was your first mistake!"

"Really?" Big Ben said turning around. "You mean you have more to cry about?"

"Hell yeah I do bitch." Smooth said walking up to his face. "Cause that's your second mistake."

"Second?" Big Ben asked Smooth. "I don't even remember what the first fucking mistake was but go on."

"See," Smooth said reaching for his waist. "You think you talking to a bitch ass nigga like I won't shoot you in your fucking face?"

"Look here you little disrespectful peace of shit." Big Ben said crossing his arms. "I ain't gonna kill you because you one of Nick's people but could you just shut the fuck up?"

"What?" Smooth said as the gun came from his waist, nigga you got me all the way fucked up."

Big Ben reached in his pocket and pulled a hundred bands out handing it to Smooth then turned to walk in the store.

"That should shut you the fuck up for a little bit." Big Ben said once he made it to the door. "Just earn your money like a good little soldier."

Smooth gave him a cold look before he put the money in his pocket then went back to the pump as they went in the store.

"This shit stupid." Smooth said when he got in the car. "This nigga gonna get us all killed for this bullshit."

He pulled out his phone and was about to dial Nick when the car door opened and everyone got back in so he started the car then followed the van leaving the gas station.

"Where the fuck we going? Smooth asked James as he rolled a blunt. "And why the fuck we in Houston?"

"Man, we going to the safe house in Stop Six." JuJu said from the back seat. "Big Ben already got everything set up so just sit back and get this paper."

"You think so?" Smooth said turning up the music. "Ya'll niggas crazy if you think we gonna live behind this."

It took almost an hour to get the safe house. They pulled up to a house close to the airport and parked in the driveway then Big Ben and J Rich jumped out and ran to the back. A few minutes later the garage door opened to J Rich standing by the door waving everyone in.

"I think we stopped moving." MaStarPeace whispered as she tried to move her hands. "Anyone, anywhere close to getting loose yet?"

"Hell, I honestly think they getting tighter." Yetta said in a painful voice. "What about you Kesha?"

She didn't respond so MaStarPeace rolled over.

"Kesha!" She yelled, moving closer. "You better wake the fuck up!"

They still got no response as the van started moving again. Yetta pushed Kesha with her foot a few times then rolled her onto her back.

"Well, it looks like she's still breathing." Yetta said looking at her stomach. "So, I guess that's a good thing."

"Girl my hand's almost free." MaStarPeace said rolling around the van. "I just gotta twist a few more times."

Big Ben turned around and watched her as she tried to get out of the zip tie. He smiled at her attempt.

"I knew from the start that you would be a problem." Big Ben said turning back around in his seat. "But don't worry, we almost home baby."

"Naw Boss.' J Rich said pulling in the driveway. "We already here."

"That's good because she already turning into a problem." Big Ben said pointing to the back. "Why is it always the smallest one?"

"You kidding me right?" J Rich said putting the car in park. "Nigga, that's Bam sister so don't sleep on the giant."

"Giant?" Big Ben looked confused. "What the fuck is that supposed to mean?"

"Man, you niggas just don't know." J Rich said opening his door. "And let's hope you don't have to find out."

"Bro, where the fuck is she gonna run to?" Big Ben said opening his door. "And they don't even know where the fuck we at."

"It don't matter where we at, Bossman." J Rich said. "In they minds, everywhere is Killa City."

Big Ben turned and looked at MaStarPeace as her hands got free before they both got out the van and walked to the back door.

"It's about time." MaStarPeace said when the zip tie slid off of her hands. "I finally got out of that bullshit."

She went over to help Yetta once they got out the van. She seen how tight her zip ties were so she started looking around the van for something to cut them with but seen nothing she could use but a rusty box cutter that barely opened.

"Fuck it." She said gripping the rusty blade. "Guess this will have to do."

She went over to Yetta and put the blade between the zip tie then pulled up as hard as she could until it broke.

She went to cut Kesha's loose next. Yetta grabbed her arms and laid her head on her lap.

"Kesha?" Yetta said slapping her face. "Wake your ass up girl."

"What the fuck are you doing Yetta?" MaStarPeace said moving towards the door. "We gotta get ready to run."

"Ready for what?" Yetta said shaking her head. "I'm not ready to die, MaStarPeace?"

"Why you talking like that?" MaStarPeace said looking at her. "These pussies not gonna kill shit."

"Girl, we can't fight all of them by ourselves." Yetta said with a low voice. "And they will kill us if we try it so sit the fuck down."

"Bitch please." MaStarPeace said still holding the box cutter. "These dumbass niggas ain't gone do shit but lock us the fuck back up."

"Why is it you always gotta be the tough one?" Yetta said looking at her sideways. "Because now ain't the time to be Billy Bad Ass, MaStarPeace!"

"And why the fuck you always have to be the weak one Yetta?" MaStarPeace said rolling her eyes. "Now, why don't you shut the fuck up and grab something to fight with?"

Before Yetta could respond the doors on the van unlocked so MaStarPeace turned and put one hand on the door as she held the box cutter in the air.

19

When the doors opened, she swung fast striking Big Ben in the face then kicked J Rich as she jumped out of the van and took off running.

"Ahhh!" Big Ben yelled holding his shirt to his face. "Go get that bitch!"

Everyone started running after her except Smooth. He leaned on the van and watched as she made it to the end of the block before JuJu caught her in the middle of the street.

"Now why in the pickles and soda would you do that little girl?" JuJu asked pulling her back to the house, and how far did you think you would get?"

"Let me the fuck go bitch ass nigga!" MaStarPeace said trying to pull away. "You know my name and who the fuck I am?"

"I know exactly who you are and if I could I would" Juju said looking at her. "But I can't do that girl. Plus, your people some bitches."

"Yeah, we gonna see about that." MaStarPeace whispered as he pushed her back to the house. "And I hope I get to pull the trigger."

They made it back to the van as Smooth was getting off of it. He reached over and grabbed MaStarPeace from JuJu then gave him a mean ass look.

Juju moved away as Smooth walked past him towards the van and helped her inside. He closed the door then turned around and faced the others.

"Ain't nobody hurting these girls!" Smooth yelled in Juju face. "This supposed to be fucking business and yall already fucking up."

Big Ben was in the house wiping his face when he heard Smooth yelling outside. He turned to look at J Rich as he grabbed a towel and wiped his face.

"Who the fuck does this nigga think he is?" Big Ben said putting down the towel. "I'm about tired of his shit."

"The way it sounds he the nigga in charge." J Rich said laughing hard. "Like you working for him and shit."

"Well, I guess it's time to show him just who is in charge around here." Big Ben said laughing. "Hand me my phone off the table."

"Who the fuck could you possibly be calling right now?" J Rich said giving him the phone. "Obviously, we got shit to handle."

"Don't even trip." Big Ben said taking the phone. "Just sit back and watch the Big show."

J Rich laughed as they both headed outside and walked over to the van.

Pain was in the parking lot sitting in his car outside the pool hall when his phone started ringing. He looked at the phone and didn't recognize the number but decided to answer anyway.

"You have got to be shitting me." Pain said when he seen Big Ben's face on his FaceTime. "How in the fuck did you get my number?"

"Now is that any way to talk to your new boss?" Big Ben said looking at Pain Loc. "I think it's time for you to start showing some fucking respect."

"Mane, fuck you, bitch." Pain said hitting his blunt. "I'm gonna kill you anyway. What the fuck you want?"

"You got my money yet?" Big Ben asked.

"Bitch, I got plenty of money." Pain said. "Why don't you come take it from me and let my sister go you bitch ass nigga?"

"Oh, so you obviously still think this is a game." Big Ben said walking towards the van. "I guess I gotta show yo dumb ass that I mean business."

Big Ben walked over to the van as Smooth stood in front of the door. He pushed Big Ben's hand away when he tried to open the door.

"Get your ass the fuck out of the way." Big Ben said looking at Smooth. "I ain't got time for your bullshit."

"I don't know what you thinking about doing but it ain't happening dogg." Smooth said tapping his waist. "I promise I will light your ass up."

"Oh, I see your bitch ass not even in charge." Pain said laughing through the phone. "Just put the boss on the phone and shut the fuck up."

"Ok." Big Ben said handing the phone to Smooth. "Here you go boss."

Big Ben handed the phone to Smooth then turned and looked at J Rich. Smooth looked at the phone and was about to say something when Big Ben put a gun to his head and pulled the trigger. Big Ben laughed as his body fell to the ground with the phone still in his hand.

J Rich stepped over Smooth as he opened the door to the girls sitting in the corner. He laughed as he reached down and grabbed the phone out of Smooth's hand giving it back to Big Ben.

"Now that we got that out the way are there any more questions about who the fucking boss is?" Big Ben said looking at Pain. "Or does another example need to be made?"

"Bitch ass nigga I hate to tell you but that shit don't shake my sensors." Pain said laughing. "That's just one less person I gotta kill to get to you."

"This nigga still talking shit." Big Ben said as he stroked his beard. "Let me try a different approach."

He turned the phone around until the camera faced the inside of the van so Pain could who was inside.

"Aye don't trip yall." Pain yelled through the phone. "We gonna handle this shit and get yall home."

"Obviously not since I gave yall a time limit to deliver my money and it ain't in my account yet." Big Ben said. "But that's because you think I'm playing with you bitches."

He handed the phone to J Rich as he reached in his pocket for the cloth. J Rich turned the phone towards him.

"You see this new scar on my face Pain Loc?" Big Ben said pointing at his face. "See this is a product of you and these bitches not taking me serious thinking you're tougher than me and gonna get away without paying my money?"

"Man get to your fucking point nigga." Pain said irritated. "Cause I already told your bitch ass if you want the bread then come fucking get it, pussy."

Big Ben laughed hard pulling out his gun then pointing it towards the girls. He swung it from left to right aiming at every girl laughing as he seen what he thought was fear in their eyes.

"Nigga you ain't that got damn stupid." Pain said looking at his sister. "But be a fool and pull that trigger."

Big Ben lowered his hand as he contemplated what Pain just said then he heard a female pop off.

"Put it down like a good little pussy." She spoke. "And recognize who the fuck you fucking with."

He looked in her eyes right before he pulled the trigger hitting her in the head throwing her body against the van. Everyone stood looking lost as Big Ben reached over and grabbed the phone from J Rich.

"You bitches have eight hours to send my fucking money." Big Ben said smiling. "Don't try me again."

He hung up the phone then turned and walked towards the house stopping when he made it to the door.

"Get them bitches out of the van and lock they ass in the basement." Big Ben yelled. "And bury those body's deep in the ground."

James and Juju grabbed Smooth as J Rich climbed in the van to pick up MaStarPeace.

"I'm sorry." He said to Yetta as tears came rolling down her face. He got out the van and closed the door.

Chapter 3

Pain punched the steering wheel a few times then slammed his phone on the dashboard before throwing it on the seat. He could feel tears coming down his face as he picked up the phone. His emotions were mixed with anger and rage.

"It ain't no fucking way I'm letting this bitch ass nigga keep breathing after that bullshit." Pain said reaching for the liquor in the backseat. "Fuck I need a drink."

He took a big shot before he screamed so loud that they heard him in the pool hall. Tut Tut turned and looked outside at Pain when he heard the noise, so he got up and went outside.

Pain looked up and seen Tut Tut coming towards his car so he took another shot then put the bottle in the seat before he opened the door and got out putting his gun in his waist.

"Nephew?" Tut Tut said when he made it to the car, "What you out here doing all this screaming for?"

"Look around Unc." Pain said moving his hands around. "Please tell me how so much bullshit could happen on such a pretty ass day?"

"Look Nephew." Tut Tut started. "How many times have told I you not to let anger effect your emotions?"

"Oh, unc this ain't anger." Pain said lighting a blunt. "This shit right here is deadly."

"Man, you of all people know that nigga ain't gonna touch them girls." Tut Tut said reaching for the blunt. "He not that fucking stupid. Taking them in the first place was a mistake."

"Really?" Pain said looking at his uncle. "Then tell me why this nigga just killed one of them with me on Facetime?"

"Hold the fuck up." Tut Tut said leaning against the car. "What the fuck you mean he killed one of them?"

"Exactly what the fuck I said." Pain said taking the blunt. "The nigga called my damn phone."

"So, start from the beginning." Tut Tut asked sitting on the car. "Who the fuck called your phone?"

"The bitch ass nigga Ben." Pain said hitting the blunt. "Talking bout I better send him his money or else."

"Or else?" Tut Tut said laughing. "What was your response to that?"

"I told the bitch ass nigga to come get it!" Pain said with emphasis. "I got it all in my trunk."

"OK" Tut Tut said cutting him off. "Let me go back a step."

"What's up unc?" Pain said passing the blunt. "What you got?"

"How the fuck he get your number?" Tut Tut said looking confused. "Cause I don't even have the number to the iPhone."

"You know unc…" Pain said laughing. "That was my first fucking question too."

"Guess the nigga know one of your bitches." Tut Tut said laughing. "Cause I know he didn't get it out of your sister's phone."

"I doubt it unc, Pain said. "Even if he has her phone, he wouldn't know my number if he seen it."

"Ok." Tut Tut said throwing the blunt. "So what else happened?"

"The nigga goes outside to a van but the nigga Smooth wouldn't let him open the door."

"Smooth?" Tut Tut asked. "Who is that?"

"You know…" Pain responded. "Nick's right hand."

"Awe ok." Tut Tut said. "Go on."

"So, I made a little joke about who the real boss is and tell the nigga to put him on the phone."

"Ok." Tut Tut said. "So, what he do?"

"The nigga gave Smooth the phone but before the nigga could say anything Ben shot him in the face. "Pain said. "Then the phone dropped."

"Are you fucking serious? Tut Tut said looking at Pain. "This nigga killed Nick's right hand man right in front of you?"

"Right the fuck in front of me unc." Pain said looking at him. "Then laughed about it."

"Funky bitch." Tut Tut said. "Go on nephew."

28

"The nigga picks up the phone and looks at me for a reaction." Pain said laughing. "Then says anymore questions about who the boss is."

"Got damn!" Tut Tut said laughing. "This nigga tripping."

"So, I laugh at the clown ass nigga." Pain said. "Then he started asking about money, so I told him I got it all bitch come get it."

"So, they coming to get the bread?" Tut Tut asked, "His people on the way here?"

"Yeah right." Pain said laughing as he lit another blunt. "Them niggas wouldn't dare pull up on me."

"I didn't think so." Tut Tut said taking a drink. "Let me hit that."

"Hell yeah cause you gonna need it for the rest of this story." Pain said giving him the blunt. "Cause the shit gets worse."

"Oh shit, Tut Tut said, what else?"

"The nigga gives the phone to someone else then all I see is the inside of a van with my sister and them in the back, so I tell this nigga not to play with me like he hard."

"Then what?" Tut Tut said passing the blunt. "That's some good shit."

"He looks at me hard unc." Pain said with an attitude. "Then starts putting his gun down so I'm thinking the nigga on some bluff shit."

"Sounds like he was nephew." Tut Tut said looking at the time. "So, what the fuck was you out here yelling and screaming for?"

"That's because one of the girls in the van called him a pussy and the nigga got mad then pulled the trigger."

"No No." Tut Tut said looking at him. "He didn't hit one of them, did he?"

"I don't know unc." Pain said getting up. "The phone went down when he fired so I don't know who or what he shot but I heard them scream."

"So, you think he killed one of them? Tut Tut asked. "Or trying to make his bluff believable?"

"He wasn't bluffing unc." Pain said shaking his head. "When the phone came back up it was body laying on the floor of the van before he came back and said he wanted his money then hung up."

"Cuz, if this nigga killed anyone of them girls…" Tut Tut said getting up. "Then Gripp ain't the nigga he needs to be worried about."

"Fucking got that shit right cause mama's uncle Black on his fucking way." Pain said slowly. "And you know he ain't trying to hear shit but results."

"So Black on his way here? Tut Tut asked. "To Killa City?"

"Oh no they on the way to Houston." Pain said closing his door. "So, them niggas about to find out just who they fucking with."

"Wicked." Tut Tut said turning towards the hall.
"Let's step inside cause I need a drink."

They walked in the pool hall then walked by the bar
before Tut Tut went and sat at his table and ordered a drink.
Pain went to his office and opened a bottle pouring a
double shot before picking up the phone to call Gripp.

Chapter 4

Nine Milli and Doug D paced the hospital waiting room waiting for information on Tony's condition. Faba Abba came in with Ma Williams wondering why Tony had been in surgery for hours with no word on his condition.

They had released Skanes about an hour ago with minor injuries and he was already at the crib eating ice cream.

"Could you get me a blanket Faba?" Ma Williams said as she sat down. "And a bottle of water."

"No problem Ma." Faba said going to the desk to talk to the nurse. "Be back in a few."

He walked off as Pastor Fuller walked in the waiting area speaking to everyone as he made his way to sit beside Ma Williams. He grabbed her hand and cuffed it tightly as he hugged her shoulders.

"So, tell me sister Williams." Pastor Fuller asked. "What are they saying so far about Tony?"

"We just got here." Ma Williams said wiping her eyes. "But Doug D said he was still in surgery."

"How bad is it?" Pastor Fuller wondered. "How many times was he hit?"

"They hit him three times." Ma Williams said wiping her face. "Once in the leg, chest and shoulder plus he lost a lot of blood."

"Sister Williams, you have to know that you raised a strong young fighter." Pastor Fuller said tapping her hand. he gonna make it out of this and be stronger than before."

"I hope you're right pastor." Ma Williams said grabbing his hand. "The lord knows I'm praying for him to save my son."

"Amen sister." Pastor Fuller said putting his head down. "Let us pray."

Ma Williams held up her hand and the room got quiet as pastor said a prayer. Nine Milli's phone went off interrupting the prayer, so he instantly grabbed it and seen it was Chloe, he silenced it then stepped out the room.

Doug D was getting hungry, so he looked at his watch before walking over to talk to Ma Williams.

"I'm about to go grab something to eat." He said leaning in front of her. "Do you want anything?"

"Not right now Doug D." Ma Williams said as she looked at the Pastor. "But check with everyone else before you go."

"Brother Doug." Pastor Fuller said standing up reaching in his pocket and pulling out his wallet. "Could you get me a Dr Pepper and grab something for everyone else just in case?"

"Seriously Pastor." Doug D said laughing. "I think I can handle the drinks."

Doug D turned and walked out the waiting room laughing and didn't notice Dr. McFadden walking towards the family.

Dr McFadden opened the door and looked in to make sure she was in the right room. She seen Ma Williams sitting in the corner next to the Pastor Fuller, so she fixed her coat and was starting to walk in when Nine Milli looked up and saw her standing there. He walked over to meet her at the door.

"What's good Dr. McFadden?" Nine Milli said shaking her hand. "You look like you got some good news for me."

"Hey Nine Milli." Dr McFadden said looking at him. "I truly wish it was good news but could you come over with me so I can talk to Ma Williams please?"

"You know I will go with you anywhere." Nine Milli said holding her hand as they walked into the private waiting area. "You the one on this so called "mancation" shit."

"I been thinking about that." Dr McFadden said smiling. "But we will talk about that later."

He held the door open as she walked in and got Ma William's attention then walked over and stood behind her. Ma Williams looked up and seen who was touching her. She wiped her face then sat back in the chair as Pastor Fuller followed suit.

"Hey Dr McFadden." Ma Williams spoke with a soft tone. "Is my son finally out of surgery?"

"Yes, ma'am he is." Dr McFadden started. "But I'm sorry to have to tell you Tony died on the operating table ten minutes ago."

"Oh my God!" Ma William's screams filled the room. "What went wrong on the table?"

"Nothing went wrong Ma Williams." Dr McFadden said sitting down. "His injuries were very severe, and he lost a lot of blood. We did everything medically possible but were unable to save him."

"So, you mean to tell me my son is gone?" Ma Williams said looking at her. "My son is really dead?"

"Yes ma'am." Dr McFadden holding her free hand, "He died."

Ma Williams put her head down as Pastor Fuller got up and kneeled down beside her. Her eyes were closed tightly but her breathing was slow and steady.

"Sister Williams…" Pastor Fuller said touching her knee. "We gonna make it through this."

She raised her head to look at his face but didn't speak another word as she looked past him at Nine Milli. Nine seen the look on her face and he of all people knew from the look in her eyes exactly what was on her mind, so he reached in his pocket to grab his phone then sent Faba Abba a text message before he walked over and grabbed Ma Williams hands.

"Pastor Fuller." Nine Milli said pulling her up. "I don't mean no disrespect but I'm gonna need you to step out the way."

"But wait." Dr McFadden said touching Nine Milli. "You don't wanna see Tony before we call the funeral home?"

"Naw." Nine Milli said speaking for Ma Williams. "Matter fact, leave his body in the morgue until Kesha comes to identify him."

"So, you don't want me to release him to the funeral home?" Dr McFadden said looking at his attention go elsewhere. "Because after seventy-two hours they will start asking questions."

"It won't be that long." Nine Milli said looking at the door. "Just a day or two."

Faba Abba walked in the room making his way towards them. He noticed the look on her face when he got closer and knew what time it was. Faba went and held the door as her and Nine Milli walked past him heading to the parking lot.

When they finally made it outside Alex was standing by the car holding the door and the Baker Boys were getting into Tim's truck when he turned around seeing them. He tapped the hood to get Marcus's attention. When he turned and seen Ma William's face, he instantly knew that Tony didn't make it out of surgery.

"You have got to be kidding me Bro." Tim said looking at Marcus. "You know what this shit mean right?"

"Hell yeah I know what this shit means." Marcus said opening the door and getting in the truck. "We better get loaded up."

"Exactly." Tim said getting in. "Because shit is about to hit the fan real quick."

Tim started the truck as the limo sat in front of them. Faba Abba opened the door and got in while Nine Milli helped Ma Williams into her seat. Faba Abba turned and gave the Baker Boys a nod before he got into the limo.

Chapter 5

After the long hours on the highway, they finally made it to Houston around 11:00 pm. Doe looked up and seen the exit for MLK, so he got off and pulled into a Holiday Inn right off the highway then found a space in the back.

Once he parked Nick got out the car stretching as he looked around at the people walking the streets before he tapped Doe on the shoulder then walked off to go get the rooms.

"I need a minute Doe." Gripp said pulling out his phone. "I need to check in on Bee and the kids."

"Yadadi." Doe said opening the door. "I'm gonna run over to QuikTrip's and grab some shit."

"Aye grab me some Debbie's." Gripp said rubbing his stomach. "I think I caught a contact from you fools."

Doe laughed as he closed the door and went across the street. Gripp looked at his phone for a second before he dialed Bee.

"Mane, I love the fuck out of this city." Doe said as he lit a blunt looking around the streets. "It always feels like home when my feet hit the pavement."

He walked to the door and held it open following some young ladies in then went and made a fountain drink. He walked around looking for some chips when he heard the door open.

When he looked up, he seen two females walk in one holding the door for the other, but they had them faces.

"This shit must be déjà vu." Doe said looking at the ladies as he walked to the register. "Cause they look familiar as fuck to me."

"Bitch why is it I gotta come looking for you like you don't know to report!" Big Six said to Amanda. "You think this shit is a game or something?"

"Bitch you don't have to come looking for me." Amanda said with a sharp tone. "You could've stayed where the fuck you were at."

"Bitch this really ain't the time for your smart-ass comments." Big Six said as she motioned to Kris, where the fuck is my money?"

"Why is it you always have to be such an asshole?" Amanda said, reaching in her purse. "Take this fucking money and get out my face with all that extra."

Big Six took the money from Amanda and put it in her purse as Doe was walking to the counter. He looked over at her and recognized who she was then instantly put a smile on his face.

"My nigga Big Six!" Doe said, throwing up his arms. "What's the got damn deal?"

"I know that ain't my nigga Doahski!" Big Six said walking up to him. "How the hell you in my city without hitting me up first?"

"I didn't have time to let nobody know I was coming." Doe said as they hugged and showed love. "We here on business not personal shit."

"Business huh?" Big Six said laughing. "That's usually how it starts."

"You ain't lying." Doe said laughing with her. "But why the fuck you in here doing all this yelling and screaming at this little sexy chick?"

"Because this stupid bitch has a way of always bringing me out of my character." Big Six said as she counted the money she got from Amanda. "But this bitch always have my money with no shorts."

"Shit at the end of the day that's all that matters." Doe said as they both laughed. "But I honestly think the shit is a rush for lil mama."

"I think the bitch just like seeing me get mad." Big Six said looking at Amanda. "But how long you in the city?"

"Hopefully just a day or two. Doe said as he walked towards the door. "We just here to add to our body count ya digg."

"Not add to the body count." Big Six said intrigued. "Who the fuck you got problems with in Houston?"

"That bitch ass nigga Big Ben." Doe said grinding his teeth. "That nigga done fucked up big time."

"Oh, that nigga." Big Six said shaking her head. What the fuck he do this time?"

"The nigga took our girls." Doe said holding the door. "On the day we was trying to bury Bam."

"Yeah, that shit against the code." Big Six said as she tapped his shoulder. "Is this get back for Gripp killing his pops?"

"Maybe but that fuck nigga tried to kill Gripp first." Doe said laughing. "He just wasn't fast enough."

"You say he wasn't fast enough." Big Six said laughing. "He is a big man Doe."

"Well, the nigga should of took flying lessons." Doe said laughing hard, then maybe he would've lived after getting Gripp's cigar."

"On mamas you stupid." Big Six said laughing. "So, you got a buzz on the nigga, or do you need me to hit the streets?"

"Naw we ain't got a beat on the nigga yet." Doe said walking outside. "Hell, we literally just got here maybe ten minutes ago."

"Well shit let me know if you need us big bro." Big Six said hugging him. "You already know how we get down."

"Oh, I know and trust I will make that call if I need to." Doe said as he turned to walked back to the hotel." Just keep that phone volume up."

"Doe?" Big Six yelled stopping him in his tracks. "But I like my phone vibrating when you call."

"You still think about this dick girl?" Doe said smiling. "We ain't fucked in what four years?"

"That's how you know." Big Six said walking up to him touching his chest. "I will even bring Kris with me as a bonus."

"Oh, I see where your head at tonight." Doe said touching her ass. "Let me see what's up and I will hit you in a few."

"I will definitely be looking for that call." Big Six said turning around. "Don't be playing though cause I'm horny tonight."

"Yeah, me too but do one thing for me though." Doe said with a smirk on his face. "Bring that chick Amanda too so we can have extra fun."

"I will put that in motion." Big Six said giggling. "Go handle your business."

Doe turned back towards the hotel and started walking back towards the car. When he got closer, he could see Gripp still sitting in the car so he walked over and sat on the hood pulling a blunt out his ear.

Chapter 6

Jermaine and Lanell were getting in the truck when his stomach made a loud noise. He noticed Lanell looking at him as he put his gun in the center console and started the truck.

"I'm hungry." Jermaine said rubbing his belly. "You trying to go get something to eat or are you gonna sit there and look crazy?"

"First off, I don't like the fact you carrying that gun." Lanell said looking at his head. "And I don't know how your ass stay so skinny with all the food you eat every day."

"My gun is my business, Lanell." Jermaine said giving her a look. "Now, do you want something to eat or not because I'm not bout to play these games with you."

"Oh, you get on my last nerve." Lanell said smiling as she looked at her watch. "But I guess I could eat."

"Well look at you making grown woman decisions," Jermaine said laughing. "But I'm telling you now we going to Texas Road House."

"Well let's go boss man." Lanell said laughing with him. "You paying for it anyway."

They both laughed as Jermaine drove out of the church parking lot, turning on his music. He reached down and grabbed a bag then handed it to Lanell.

She looked inside and seen a plastic bottle and papers then sat it in her lap as she looked at him sideways.

"And what the fuck am I supposed to do with this?" Lanell said holding the bag. "Cause it's not full of money?"

"What you mean full of money?" Jermaine said laughing. "You better break that weed down and roll that shit up."

"Nigga do I look like your personal fucking roller?" Lanell said laughing. "You could of did this shit before we left."

"Yeah, I could have but then what fun would that have been?" Jermaine said laughing. "You look like you sitting in my passenger seat over there so do your job."

He stopped at a light then turned the corner as she turned downed the music. She twisted her body so that he would know she was looking directly in his face.

"Oh, so you saying I work for you now?" Lanell said with an attitude. "Then show me where them dollars at because your signature don't match the one on my paycheck."

"Why you gotta be all extra and shit? Jermaine said turning the music back up. "Roll a damn blunt."

"Oh, you a asshole," Lanell whispered as she opened the bag and grabbed the tray. "I don't even smoke the shit."

"Yeah, and that's part of your problem right there," Jermaine said laughing. "You need to hit the blunt so you can calm your ass down."

Lanell laughed hard as she poured the weed on the tray. She broke it down then tried to hand him a swisher until he looked at her crazy.

"What the hell you giving me that for?" Jermaine asked looking crazy. "Now you can't spilt a swisher?"

"Hell naw cause I don't smoke remember." She said with a smart tone. "So, break this and shut the fuck up."

"You have got to be fucking kidding me." Jermaine said taking the cigar and breaking it down. "I don't know why you over there acting like you can't do this you big headed brat."

"And that's why I can't." Lanell said laughing. "Thank you though."

Jermaine's phone rang through the Bluetooth, and he looked up and seen a number he didn't know so he let it go to voicemail.

"What bitch you ignoring today, Jermaine?" Lanell asked with a tone. "Must have been your bitch, Jessica."

They both laughed as he stopped at a red light. He looked at her and continued to laugh at her comment before he spoke.

"I don't know who the fuck that was calling." Jermaine said looking at his phone. "I'm not answering no number I don't recognize so they better text or leave a voicemail."

They both laughed as he picked up his phone but before he could check it Lanell seen the police lights flashing behind them and tapped his hand. He looked in the mirror to see they were pulling him over.

"What the fuck is this shit about?" Jermaine said pulling into a parking lot. "Cause I know I didn't do a fucking thing."

"Chill the fuck out." Lanell said squeezing his hand. "Then you shouldn't have anything to worry about." He put the truck in park and let down his window as he looked for his wallet. By the time he found it, two officers standing by his truck.

"License and registration." Officer Nelson said once he was by the window. "And keep your hands where I can see them."

"Why did you pull me over?" Jermaine asked giving him his information. "I know I wasn't speeding."

Jermaine turned to see the other officer standing by Lanell's door with his gun in his hand and turned back to look at Officer Nelson.

"Are you not gonna answer my fucking question?" Jermaine said, getting irritated. "Or are you gonna keep on with this illegal bullshit?"

"I don't have to answer a fucking thing." Officer Nelson said with an attitude. "Now how about you stop with the attitude before your dumbass end up in jail instead of just a fucking ticket."

"Whatever bro," Jermaine said sitting back in his seat. "You in charge."

"You got damn right." Officer Nelson said, turning to walk to his patrol car. "Watch them and make sure they don't move."

Lanell rolled down her window and looked at the officer's badge number as well as his face.

"So, why do you have your weapon out?" She asked in a soft voice. "We look dangerous to you or something?"

"I just do as I'm told ma'am." Officer Pitts responded looking up as his partner hold up three fingers as he came back to the truck. He holstered his weapon when his partner opened Jermaine's door.

"I'm gonna need both of you to step out of the truck." Officer Nelson said looking at him and put your hands on the vehicle."

"I ain't stepping out of shit!" Jermaine said, loud. "Your ass ain't even told me why you pulled me the fuck over and now you want me to get out my truck?"

"Yeah." Officer Nelson said laughing. "Since you put it that way."

"You know what bro?" Jermaine said looking at him, "Fuck you."

"I pulled your dumb ass over because your paper tag says January 2019." Officer Nelson replied. "And this is September 2020, but your dumb ass already know all of this because your warrant in Oklahoma County is for traffic tickets."

"Mane, you on that bullshit cuz." Jermaine said reaching in his backseat. "I have a tag right here I just ain't had time to put it on."

"That sound like a personal problem to me." Officer Nelson said laughing. "Now, get the fuck out the truck."

Jermaine looked at Lanell but didn't attempt to move or get out, so Officer Nelson reached down and snatched him out then threw him against the truck with force.

"I ain't got all day to be playing with you boy." Officer Nelson said pulling his cuffs out to put on Jermaine. "Detain her too Pitts."

"Why in the fuck am I being detained?" Lanell asked turning her head to him. "You must really hate your job."

"Also, call a tow truck Pitts." Officer Nelson said, pushing Jermaine towards the car. "Backup should be here in a few."

"Why are you having his truck towed?" Lanell asked as Pitts put cuffs on her. "When the traffic stop was faulty in the first place?"

"Because he has a warrant for his arrest." Officer Pitts replied. "And driving a nonregistered vehicle."

"Why can't I just drive his truck?" Lanell asked with a tone. "Because I have no warrants and a license?"

"That's a question you have to ask my supervisor." Officer Pitts answered. "And you can't do that until we get to the station."

Officer Nelson turned and walked away with Jermaine in front of him when Lanell looked up and seen Detective White pull up with another car behind him. He got out the car looking around the scene before he walked over to them.

"Now you ain't got to look at me like that Ms. Lanell." Detective White said smiling at her. "I just figured you might want a comfortable ride to the station."

"Detective White." Lanell said shaking her head. "You still a thirsty ass nigga I see."

Detective White laughed as he turned to say a few words to the other officer's before looking back to her.

"I got her Pitts, Detective White said grabbing her arm, lets go Lanell."

Lanell didn't say a word as he walked her to his truck and opened the front door. She turned and gave him a nasty look as she got in before he closed the door then looked at Jermaine smiling as he got in.

Detective White drove off with Officer Nelson and Pitts following as they headed to the police station when Lanell pulled out her phone and tried to make a call but White grabbed it out of her hands.

"Oh, you done really lost your damn mind I see." Lanell said looking irritated. "Give me my fucking phone."

"You will get this phone back when I give it to you." Detective White said pulling into the station. "Until then I don't wanna hear your mouth."

He walked around and opened her door to a devilish look. He stepped aside so she would have room to get out.

"Why in the fuck did your people pull us over anyway?" Lanell asked getting out of truck. "Cause I know Jermaine didn't break any traffic laws."

"You know I have no idea why they stopped him." Detective White said walking behind her as they walked in the building. "But at this point it doesn't even matter because we are here now."

"At the end of the day it's still some bullshit." Lanell said walking into the interrogation room. "So, I hope ya'll truly done talking to me."

"Let's just hope you tell us what we need." Detective White said. "And you can be home by dinner."

"Nigga please." Lanell said crossing her hands. "Do I look like a fucking bird?"

"No." Detective White said walking to the door. "But get that singing voice ready for me."

"Singing voice?" Lanell said as he said as closed the door. "See this is the type of shit I don't have time for."

Detective White walked over as Officer Nelson was putting Jermaine in another interrogation room, so he went in behind them and closed the door.

"Have a seat Jermaine." Officer Nelson said pointing at the chair. "And put your cuffs through the loop on the table."

"How long I'm gonna be in here?" Jermaine said as they were walking out the door. "And when do I get my phone call?"

They kept walking without saying a word before closing the door leaving him looking at the walls and mirror, so he started to run back everything in his head.

"I know one thing." Jermaine said to himself. "This right here is some straight bullshit."

Detective White walked over to his desk with a big smile on his face nodding at his partner knowing he was about to close his case.

"So, what's up?' Detective Dyer said grabbing his notepad. "Cause I really hope we get a confession out of these two."

"Yeah, I'm ready." Detective White said getting a pen. "We only need one of them to talk so this should be an easy one."

"I don't think it will be partner." Detective Dyer said looking at paperwork. "After reading his sheet he doesn't have any priors or a reason to talk."

"Mane this nigga gonna sing like he is fucking Neo." Detective White said opening his file. "The nervous ones always crack easily."

They both laughed as Detective Dyer got up and followed White to interrogation room one. White stopped at the window looking in on Lanell with her head on the desk then laughed as he continued walking.

When he opened the door, he could see sweat dripping from Jermaine head, so he pulled out a chair as his partner closed the door behind him.

Instead of sitting down Detective Dyer leaned against the wall as Detective White sat down looking Jermaine in the eye. The room was quiet for a minute until Jermaine finally spoke.

"Why in the fuck am I here? Jermaine asked with an attitude. "And what the fuck do ya'll want?"

"Oh, you feel like you have the right to ask questions?" Detective Dyer said still leaning. "Well, you only have the right to answer them boy."

"Excuse me." Jermaine said looking at White. "Man, you better get this bitch ass partner of yours, White."

"Now why would I do that?" Detective White said laughing. "Because he's your little brother?"

"That and because he's a bitch." Jermaine said looking at Dyer. "So, like I said what the fuck do yall want?"

"Another fucking question." Detective Dyer said laughing. "Well let's start with you telling us about Price's murder?"

"Who the fuck is Price?" Jermaine asked looking at White. "And why would I know anything about his murder?"

"How about you tell us what you know about Bam's murder?" Detective White said lighting a cigarette. "That name ring a bell in your peanut ass head?"

"You got me in here asking about Bam's murder?" Jermaine said looking confused. "Man, I don't know shit about that."

"Is that right?" Detective Dyer said with a smirk. "Well, we have a witness that says you took money and setup the whole thing."

Jermaine laughed loud enough for the whole room to notice as he looked both of them in the face then he laughed again before he spoke.

"Well, I know Lanell ain't told you no bullshit like that." Jermaine said smiling. "And if you got a witness lock me up."

White jumped out the chair fast picking Jermaine up by the shirt then pushing him against the wall. Jermaine smiling at me for tried to push him off but White pushed harder melting his body against the wall.

"Listen to me you little piece of shit!" Detective White said looking in his eyes. "I know you made the phone call and gave up the location because I already checked your phone records dummy."

He pushed Jermaine to the other side of the room before he turned around and slammed the door as he walked out the room.

Jermaine got up and fixed his clothes the best he could before he went to sit back in the chair then looked up at Detective Dyer when his stomach made a loud noise.

"You alright over there big bro?" Detective Dyer said standing up, "you need a bathroom or something?"

"Hell naw, I don't need to go to no bathroom nigga," Jermaine said laughing, "I'm hungry as fuck and need some fucking food."

"You know that nigga ain't about to let me bring you no food up in here," Detective Dyer said looking at him, "unless you about to talk."

"I'll talk if you bring me some food," Jermaine said shrugging his shoulders, "and if you don't I'm calling auntie to tell on your ass."

Jermaine sat back in his chair looking at the mirror as Detective Dyer opened the door. He could hear someone crying and screaming for they mama, so he turned back to Jermaine.

"See what I'm saying," Detective Dyer said looking at Jermaine, "that tough guy shit don't work in here big bro."

Detective Dyer closed the door laughing as he walked over to Officer Harris standing by the glass to interrogation room three.

"What's up Mike?" Detective Dyer said pointing, "what the hell is wrong with your collar crying like that?"

"Who Mr. Hannibal?" Mike said laughing hard, "say he wanna call his momma because he not supposed to be here."

"Hell, none of them are supposed to be here, Dyer said turning around, "what is he charged with anyway?"

"For a failure to appear warrant, Mike said laughing, "hell I was gonna let the kid go but we all enjoying the show."

"Sounds like someone thinks he going to jail tonight," Dyer said laughing, "the room does it every time."

"Oh you should of seen him before the cuffs went on," Mike said laughing, "he was Billy the gangster then got soft as soon as they locked."

"I bet his ass did," Dyer said still laughing, "so you gonna let him call his mama or what?"

"Here in a few I will," Mike said looking at the time, "he can keep crying until then."

"You cold as hell Mike, Dyer said, "just ruthless for no reason."

"Naw brother," Mike said looking at him, "just tired of people thinking a few tears will make a difference."

"You not lying on that one," Dyer said, "I will get with you later."

Dyer turned and headed to White's desk and seen he wasn't there, so he wrote a note and left it before he headed to the lobby.

Chapter 7

Gripp got out the car looking at the parking lot as he hung up the phone. He took a deep breath as Nick was walking back to the car.

"Mane it ain't nothing like Houston," Gripp said looking at Nick, "it's like a whole vibe of its own."

"Man, this hot ass, humid ass air," Nick said laughing as he wiped his head, "fuck that I'd rather be in Miami right now."

"Boy, you young niggas don't know shit," Gripp said shaking his head, "you will learn to enjoy this type of shit one day."

Doe walked up hitting a blunt as they were talking so he passed it to Nick then leaned against the car as Gripp walked around it.

"So, what type of rooms your cheap ass get us?" Doe asked reaching for the keys, "cause I'm ready to lay it down."

"Shit you ain't the only one," Gripp said yawning and stretching, "we got a long ass day ahead of us tomorrow."

"Hopefully we don't," Nick said passing them keys, "and nigga I got suites you asshole."

"So, since these basically your bitches," Doe asked taking his key, "how you think they gonna play it?"

"Well since them niggas are so fucking predictable," Nick said laughing, "all we gotta do is follow the map."

"I can dig that," Doe said throwing the blunt, "let's get upstairs."

They walked in the hotel and stood in front of the elevator door waiting for it to open. Once it did, they hopped on as Nick pressed the button for the seventh floor.

They rode up in silence until Doe's phone started beeping. He looked at it as the elevator stopped and seen a message from Pain. He texted, 'Let me handle this business then I will hit you,' then put his phone in his pocket.

"Yadadi!" Doe said when the doors finally opened, "you niggas rest up and I will get at you in the AM."

Doe got off the elevator and headed to his room. He stopped and looked to make sure Gripp got in before he walked in his room and closed the door.

He pulled out his phone and texted Big Six.

'What's good girl.? You still trying to come thru?'

'Hell yeah, we are. What hotel you at?'

'I'm at the hotel across the street from the store. Who is we?'

'Everyone you asked for baby.'

'Yadadi! I'm in 723'

Doe put his phone down then went to turn on the shower after throwing his clothes on the floor. By the time he was done he heard a knock at the door, so he put on a towel and grabbed his gun before going to answer it.

Nick walked out his room headed to get some ice and grab a drink from the machine when he looked up and seen three chicks get off the elevator looking scrumptious, so he watched as they made their way down the hall stopping in front of Doe's door.

Nick's hood mentality kicked in quick as he walked up to them pulling out his gun pointing it directly at Big Six. Amanda looked at the side of Nick's face for a second before she pulled out her .380 and pointed it at that same spot.

"See, putting a gun to my bosses head, normally doesn't get this much attention," Amanda said pushing her gun, "but you fine so I will hear you out before I kill you."

"Man, you bitches got balls in Houston," Nick said looking at Amanda, "you must not know who the fuck I am."

"Naw I don't," Amanda said smiling, "why don't you enlighten me."

"His name is Nick from Arkansas," Kris said cutting him off, "they call him Knock Out."

"See somebody know they shit," Nick said smiling at Kris, "how you know that girl?"

"Because Campbell's my cousin," Kris responded, "and because you're an enemy of Killa City."

"Yeah, I was until our paths crossed," Nick said, "now we in this shit together."

"We will see about that," Big Six said knocking on the door, "cause if Doe say something different, I'm gonna tell her to decorate the walls with that pretty ass face."

Big Six took a deep breath when Doe opened the door with a gun standing in a towel. Her pussy instantly got wet as she reached and touched his chest.

"Man, what the fuck going on out here nigga?" Doe asked looking at Nick, "why the fuck you got the heat on the ladies?"

"Bro, you know where we come from," Nick said putting down his gun, "it's female hitters everywhere."

"I can dig that," Doe said grabbing Big Six's hand, "but these right here are invited guests.

You hear that," Big Six said walking in, "invited guest"?

"Oh, I got you nigga," Nick said turning around, "have fun with all of that."

"Aye Doe," Amanda said putting her gun back in her purse, "let me bring him to the party."

"Really," Doe asked looking confused, "why you want this jelly faced ass nigga in here"?

"The nigga look like he can slang some dick," Amanda said grabbing his belt buckle, "and I'm trying to find out."

When they all walked in the room Nick sat on the desk by the TV. Doe went into a separate room then came out with a robe on and sat in a chair by the bed.

Big Six walked over and kissed his chest then looked at Kris. She came over and kissed Doe then kissed Big Six on the lips before standing up and looking at Amanda.

Amanda came over and started taking off Kris's clothes until she was standing naked in front of Doe. Kris turned around and crawled on the bed making sure he could see every part of her ass in front of him.

Doe reached over and slapped her ass then turned to look at Big Six, so she looked at Amanda. She smiled as she walked over and took off Big Six's clothes, throwing them on the floor.

Doe kissed her leg as she crawled on the bed with Kris spreading her legs in front of her. As Kris started to lick her thighs, Nick walked over and started taking off Amanda's clothes then pointed at the bed as he threw them on the floor.

Amanda got on her knees in front of Doe then put her hands on Kris's ass cheeks spreading them wide before she put her tongue deep in her pussy. Kris moaned loud and bit Big Six as Amanda licked her inner pussy.

Kris spread her legs and pushed her ass higher in the air so Amanda could hit her clit with her tongue. They all started moaning as they came one after the other.

Big Six got up and walked to the back of the bed then laid on the floor as she pulled Amanda's pussy down and sat it on her tongue. Amanda came instantly as her body started to shake and her orgasm splashed Big Six's face.

Doe slapped Big Six on the ass before he picked her up off the floor. He took her hand then reached and grabbed Kris off the bed.

"Yall have fun," Doe said walking in the bedroom, "we gonna take our party in here."

Amanda watched them as they went in and left the door open before she turned and put her attention on Nick grabbing his hands and pushing him onto the bed.

She unbuttoned his pants and slid them to the floor then pulled his dick through the hole of his boxers before she took him deep in her mouth wetting every inch of him until her lips touched his stomach.

Nick leaned his head back and moaned as she sucked him slow and deep as she grabbed is hands putting them on the back of her head. She raised up and looked at him.

"Show me how you like this dick sucked," Amanda said licking her lips, "and don't be scared to make me deep throat it."

Nick smiled as he put his dick back in her mouth moving her head to his beat. Kris turned and looked at Amanda sucking on Nick, so she walked over to give her a hand while Doe was fucking Big Six from the back.

"Where you going girl?" Doe said to Big Six as she tried to run. "Get over here.

"Oh fuck!" Big Six screamed as Kris walked in the other room. "You fucking the shit out me!"

Kris got down beside Amanda then tapped her on the ass. When she looked up, she smiled and handed Nick's dick to Kris so she could get to work.

Kris played with the head teasing Nick as his eyes rolled in his head. Amanda got up and walked in the room and pushed Doe making him fall on Big Six.

"Girl why did you do that?" Doe laughed, "I was in motion with that pussy."

"I saw that," she said crawling on top of him, "that made me want some of this dick even more."

Amanda put Doe inside her, barely breathing, as she slid slowly down his dick. Big Six put her hands on Doe's chest leaning over sucking Amanda's nipples as she rode the wave.

Kris got up and crawled on the bed then grabbed Nick's dick as she glided herself down. She slowly swayed her hips moving in circles until she heard a phone ring and seen Doe jump off the bed.

"Pain Loc," Doe said breathing heavy when he answered the phone, "cuz I'm kinda tied up right now."

"Well untie yourself," Pain said sounding worried, "and tell that girl to bounce."

"Damn cuz you tripping," Doe looked at Big Six, "then what im gone tell the other two"?

"Oh, shit you got three my nigga," Pain said excited, "well I sholl hate to interrupt that good shit bro but I'm trying to give you an update on Tony."

"Hold up Amanda," Doe said stopping her, "now what the fuck you just say nigga?"

"Bro, you heard me right," Pain poured himself a drink, "clear your room and hit me back."

Doe looked at the phone for a second before he hung up. Big Six stood up and walked over to him.

"What's the deal Doe," Big Six said touching his hand, "you good"?

"Aye, my bad but all yall gotta go," Doe said picking up clothes, "we can finish this another time."

No one questioned him as they put on their clothes. The ladies waved as they headed out the door. Nick came and shook Doe's hand before he walked out closing the door behind him.

Doe sat in the quiet room thinking about Tony laying in that hospital fighting for his life with his girl and sister fighting for theirs, so he got up and poured a drink from the bar then picked up his phone to call Pain.

"What up Doe?" Pain answered on the first ring. "Man it's been a very fucked up day."

"Bro it's been a fucked up weekend," Doe responded picking up his glass, "I can't wait to kill these bitches for the disrespectful shit they pulled."

"You ain't lying my nigga," Pain said in a tone, "but for you it's about to get worse."

"What the fuck you mean it's about to get worse," Doe took a sip of his drink, "what the fuck done happened now"?

"I hope you got a blunt," Pain hesitated before going into his explanation, "a fat one."

As Doe listened, he could feel the tension in his body getting tighter with every word and by the time Pain was done explaining he was pouring his second drink, so he waited and took a deep breath before he spoke.

"So, you mean to tell me that this nigga shot one of our girls and you don't know who the hell it is?" Doe asked with a buzz in his voice, "I know that shit eating you more than me."

"You know it is bro, but the nigga dropped the phone before the shot went off."

"So, who you think it is bro, cause the way you talking it was Kesha."

"Honestly I don't know my nigga," Pain said thinking, "but I do know it ain't my sister."

"And how the fuck you know that when you said you didn't see shit?"

"Cause, I would feel that shit bro, Pain responded with a tear, "you know me and my sister that close."

"Yeah, that's true," Doe agreed, "you two are close as shit but that means now we gotta get to them fast."

"Fast as hell bro," Pain said lighting a blunt, "I don't want another surprise call from that bitch ass nigga."

"I doubt you get another call," Doe said putting on a shirt, "I don't think the nigga that stupid."

"I think he is bro but wait till I get my hands on that bitch ass nigga."

"You won't get the chance to if I get to that nigga first," Doe responded through clenched teeth, "cause I promise that nigga gonna feel every bit of me."

"I can dig that shit," Pain laughed, "you make sure Gripp is straight?"

"Them niggas went to they rooms already," Doe said, "matter fact the nigga Nick just left from out of here a minute ago."

"Oh, you let the nigga in on the fun huh," Pain asked, "acting like best friends and shit."

"Nigga fuck you," Doe said laughing, "I can go wake them niggas up."

"Naw, don't do that," Pain replied quickly, "let them niggas rest because I got more news for you."

"What's up," Doe said sitting up, "what else you got?

"You ain't gonna like this shit nigga," Pain said pouring another drink, "but the nigga Tony didn't make it cuz."

The phone was quiet for a minute before Pain heard a loud banging noise on the other end, so he just kept sipping until he heard Doe pick the phone back up.

"Mane, I thought yall said them was baby shots cuz, what the fuck went wrong"?

"Mane I just got the call bro; I wasn't there to talk to Dr. McFadden."

"Bro, you just activated the old me," Doe said grabbing his gun, "I'm about to hit these streets."

"You not waiting on Gripp and Nick bro, you going out by yourself?"

"Hell yeah, I am bro!" Doe said taking a deep breath, "Tony was one of the first niggas I watched grow into a gangsta so I'm out this bitch!"

"You be careful cuz," Pain said with a warning, "do everything stupid but smart as fuck."

"Already cuz," Doe said laughing, "no fires in this city."

Doe hung up and grabbed his gun before he walked out the room. He pressed the button on the elevator then pulled out his phone and texted Black as he waited to see where he was. Black texted back and said he was in the parking lot of the hotel beside his car.

"How the fuck is he in the parking lot," Doe said looking at the text, " and how the fuck does he know where we at"?

He got on the elevator, rode to the bottom floor then stepped into the quiet lobby looking around before he went outside. He lit a blunt as a navigator pulled up in front of him and rolled the window down. When Doe looked through the window, he could see Black in the driver's seat and laughed as he opened the door and got in.

"What's up Big Bro," Doe said shaking Black's hand, "how the fuck you know where we was at?"

"Shit, I hacked Gripp phone and got his location," Black said pointing at his laptop, "you know how I get down nigga."

"Well, why the fuck you haven't found the girls yet?" Doe asked as they drove out the parking lot, "Your system getting as old as your ass?"

"You stupid," Black said laughing, "but that's what I was doing before you walked out and I got a pin on Kesha's phone."

"You got a pin?" Doe said looking at the laptop, how far away is that from where we at now?"

"Looks like twenty-one miles," Black said tapping the laptop, "I was about to go before you texted."

"Shid you ain't got to do that," Doe said sitting back, "cause now you got some backup."

Black looked at the GPS as they pulled out of the parking lot and headed to the highway while Doe smoked his blunt. Black was quiet and concentrated on the road when Doe offered him the blunt, but he refused and pointed to the glove box. Doe opened it and two Glocks fell out. He laughed at that then he passed them to Black.

"Oh, my black babies," Black said grabbing his guns, "sorry I had yall in the dark so long."

"What the fuck you doing? Doe said looking at Black, "Nigga I know you ain't talking to your guns now?"

"These ain't just guns my boy," Black said putting them on his lap, "these is family and they have killed a lot of people for me."

"The hoes look brand new." Doe grabbed one and loaded the chamber. "You sure you didn't catch a contact?"

"Yeah, nigga I'm sure," Black said laughing, "I just take care of my bitches."

Doe laughed as the GPS started talking letting them know they were almost to their destination. When they pulled into the quiet neighborhood passing the houses, they saw a big shed sitting in a field.

"I bet they in there," Black said pointing, "we gonna park over here and tool up."

Black parked in front of a house. They both got out and walked to the back as he opened the truck making Doe smile as he looked down at the artillery in front of him. "I see you ready for war. I'm gonna enjoy this shit."

"Yeah, I stay ready for everything," Black said grabbing 2 shotguns, "let's go get these bitches."

They walked slowly on the side of a house towards the shed till Doe stopped and held up his hand pointing at the men standing behind the barn, so they pushed their bodies against the house.

"You think we should play it cool," Black asked looking around, "or just run in and blast their ass?"

"See that's the problem with you old heads," Doe said laughing, "yall ain't got no patience."

"What the hell is that supposed to mean," Black asked laughing, "cause I got patience nigga."

"Naw you don't," Doe said laughing, "because it's most likely more than them niggas here so if we run in blasting them niggas gonna get the drop on us."

"So, what do you suggest Grasshopper," Black laughed, "juke and fake?"

"That's exactly what I'm saying," Doe said looking around, "go find you a spot and I'm gonna go introduce myself."

"It's a bet, give me about 5 minutes then go," Black told him before walking away.

He walked off and disappeared within seconds as Doe pulled out his gun popping one in the chamber then put it back and started walking with the .357 in his hand towards the back of the shed.

When he got closer, he could see that they were digging a hole behind the shed. He walked up slowly getting close before he put his gun to the back of Kyle's head.

"What the fuck," Kyle said turning around, "nigga do you know who I am"?

"You must not know who you fucking with or what the fuck we could do to you," Ryan said reaching for his gun.

"I do know what I'm gonna do if you touch that pistol," Doe said pointing one gun at him while putting another one on Kyle, "so you could be smart or be stupid your choice."

"Yeah homie I don't think so, I think that's a choice that you gonna make," Juju said putting the gun to Doe's head.

"Bitch ass Juju, I was really hoping I would be the one to kill you," Doe said laughing.

"Man, I know you not still pissed about that damn soup from the yard, Juju said laughing, "dog that was over ten years ago."

"And that should let you know how much you pissed me the fuck off with that bullshit, Doe said mugging him, "that was some bitch ass shit Juju."

"Whatever Nig…

Before Juju could get his sentence out Ryan saw the beam right as the bullet went through his head making his body fall beside the hole. Juju turned around fast to see where it came from before he caught the next one in the leg.

Doe stood still with his guns pointed at Kyle as he stood looking down at Juju. "What's that bullshit you was talking, you lucky I don't blast your bitch ass now."

"Fuck you, nigga, Juju said spitting, "whoever shot me in the leg gonna catch a bullet in the face."

"I doubt that," Doe said laughing, "now where the fuck our girls at bitch?"

"That nigga said girls, what fucking girls you talking bout?" Juju said laughing back at him.

"Oh, I see you got jokes, just keep laughing bitch."
Doe thought about killing Juju but decided against it and
pulled the trigger shooting Juju in his other leg making him
scream loud as Black walked up and stood behind him.

"So, you still don't know what girls I'm talking
about, or do I need to start shooting your arms?"

"Hold that thought, Doe," Black said tapping his
shoulder, "let me ask the little light skin nigga over here."

"That nigga called you light skin," Doe laughed
hard, "go ahead and see what he got to say, Black."

Black looked over at Kyle hard before he reached
down and pulled him up to his feet then looked in his eyes
hard before he finally spoke.

"I'm not as patient as my nigga Doe," Black said
holding his shirt, "so I'm only gonna ask a few questions
and if I like all your answers, I won't kill you."

"Sounds simple enough to me," Kyle said looking
at Juju, "what you want to know?"

"Where the fuck are my nieces and what the fuck
are you digging a hole for?" Black asked with force.

"I don't know where they took them two girls and
the hole is for the bodies in the shed."

"Bodies?" Doe asked pushing his gun to Kyle's
head, "what fucking bodies?"

"Some nigga and a chick," Kyle said looking in
Doe's eyes, "look man I'm just a soldier and I didn't even
know these people, cuz."

"Well, I guess you should of did some research before you took the assignment now you in the middle of some bullshit." Doe said looking at him.

"Where the fuck your boss at, cause I know you the bitch's driver so you gotta know something?" Black said cocking his other gun.

"Like he said we don't know where the fuck they went, why don't you ask the dead nigga!" JuJu yelled.

Juju pointed at Ryan as Doe started laughing then he put his attention back on him putting his gun on the top of Juju's head.

"So do I need to repeat the question," Doe said slowly, "or do you understand the assignment?"

"Oh, I understand that you can suck my dick and that soup tasted like shit," Juju said spitting on the ground.

Doe pulled the trigger three times before Black pushed his arm to get his attention. He looked at Black and shook his head then checked his gun.

"My bad bro," Doe said laughing, "but I been wanting to kill that bitch ass nigga."

They both started laughing as they looked at Kyle sitting on the ground. Black thought long and hard but decided the boy could be useful.

"Get up and show me the bodies," Black said looking at the shed, "then you gonna call your boss and tell him what happened then ask for a ride or location."

"Whatever you need, just don't kill me."

Kyle said turning around.

They walked around to the front of the shed and hit a light switch on the outside before Kyle opened the door. They walked in seeing nothing but tools and a safe. Doe looked at Black giving him a nod when he knew they had the same thought. Kyle pointed at the safe then started walking towards it and put in the code to open it. He grabbed a remote and hit another button that opened a door behind the safe and then pointed into the room.

"The bodies in there," Kyle said," "and the only thing I was told is to make sure they were buried deep."

Doe started to walk when Black grabbed his arm and pulled him back motioning for him to stay and watch so Doe did as he said.

Black went in and looked around the whole room to make sure it was empty before he looked on the floor at the two bodies under sheets. He walked over slowly and kneeled down over the first sheet pulling it back.

When he did, he closed his eyes, made a cross as he seen Smooth laying there with a bullet in his face knowing Smooth stayed solid till the end.

"Damn lil buddy," Black said as he put the sheet back and got up, "I hate it had to be you."

He walked over to the other sheet and took a deep breath before he kneeled down. He waited a few seconds before he pulled back the sheet and looked at her body. His eyes instantly watered at the site of her laying with a hole in her head. He reached down and touched her face. More tears fell as he stood up and walked back to the door.

"Come on Doe, you need to see this."

Doe looked at Black and saw the difference in his walk as he walked past Kyle and stepped out the way so he could walk into the room.

He saw the bodies lying on the floor under the sheets, as he got closer he bent down and moved the sheet revealing Smooth first. He stopped for a second then walked further into the corner and saw her body on the floor.

Tears instantly came from his face as he fell to the floor. He sat on the floor for a minute before he got up and wrapped the sheets back around then picked up her body as he turned back towards the door. He was walking out of the room and headed to the door of the shed when he stopped at the door and said something to Black.

"I'm taking her Vance so he can get her home bro, Doe said in an angry voice, "yall make sure this shit gets cleaned up."

"I got you," Black said handing him the keys, "you gonna take Smooth's body too?"

"Yeah, I think I am," Doe said calming his voice, that's Nick homeboy and he died protecting them girls."

"I can dig it, go get the fucking body," Black said looking at Kyle.

Kyle went into the room as Doe walked out to the truck and put her in the backseat then he opened the truck so Kyle could put smooth in then closed it, got in the SUV and drove off without saying a word.

Kyle turned and saw Black in the backyard walking around so he went back there. Black threw him a shovel and pointed at the hole, he jumped in and continued digging.

After about an hour Black said the hole was deep enough so Kyle stopped digging and then jumped out of the hole. He looked at Black standing in front of Juju.

"Help me put this nigga in first," Black said holding Juju's arms, "then we will work on the other bitch."

"And after that I guess you gonna make me fill this fucking hole back up," Kyle asked wiping his sweat, "can I at least get some damn water first?"

"I'm gonna give you a break in a few," Black said looking at him, "and I'm gonna fill up the hole."

"Damn man you alright," Kyle said grabbing Juju's legs, "let's hurry up and get this shit over with."

They grabbed Juju and threw him in the hole and laughed when his body made a loud clump sound. They turned and grabbed Ryan rolling him in the hole.

Kyle was turning around to pick up the shovel when he felt Black wrap his arm around his neck and pick him up off the ground. Black choked him until his body stopped moving then dropped him in the hole. He picked up the shovel and started shoveling the dirt back into the hole.

When he was done, he walked back into the shed and picked up the keys and phone he saw laying on the floor then walked outside and hit the button.

The lights on a Ford truck blinked so he walked towards it and got in, started it and watched as it instantly connected to the phone he had. He could see now that it was Juju's phone, so he went through the call log and texts looking for any leads on his next move. Finding nothing that jumped out at him he went to the location history and seen that Juju was at an address in South Houston for over three hours before coming here.

He turned on the lights and looked around the truck and seen blood on the backseat, so he put that address in the GPS then turned on an old school station as he drove off.

Chapter 8

Doe pulled over on the side of the freeway and pulled out his phone dialing Pain as he rolled a blunt. When Pain answered he turned and looked at her in the backseat before he spoke.

"I got her and Smooth cuz, I'm taking them to Vance so he can get them home then link back up with Black and continue the hunt."

"So, who is it cuz," Pain asked pouring a drink, "which one took the bullet?"

"The last one you would expect, cuz," Doe said lighting the blunt, "don't look like she suffered though."

"I fucking knew it, Pain said throwing a cup, now how the fuck we gonna explain why these niggas still breathing after this shit."

"I don't know bro, but I did kill that nigga Juju."

"Oh yeah," Pain said with some relief, "the nigga didn't tell you where they at?"

"Naw bro the nigga didn't give up shit and it was two other niggas there but neither spoke anything relevant."

"Shiddd they never do, plus that nigga Juju a soldier so he would've never been a snitch." Pain replied.

"Well, I know that now," Doe said laughing, the nigga died with that truth."

"Hell naw, did you already call Gripp?"

"Hell naw," Doe said fast, "I'm just gonna smoke with my girl and enjoy this ride home."

"That sounds like a plan bro, cause that's what the fuck I would do."

"Righteous," Doe said, "are you gonna call Ma Williams?"

"No sir I'm not," Pain said coughing, "when you make it back, we will let everyone know but until then we at war and not showing no weakness."

"Already so what's going on in the city," Doe asked changing the subject, "somebody making everybody pick-ups?"

"Now you know I'm gonna stay on top of the money my nigga, making sure no one is short."

"Who doing the pick-ups?" Doe asked, "Cause I need them to go see Shine and pick up a package for me.

"I'm doing them personally, I told you no shorts today." Pain responded.

"Well, swing by Shine spot on 23rd for me and put that shit in the pool hall until I get back," Doe asked.

"I got you bruh," Pain said, "anything else you need me to handle in the meantime?"

"Naw, I'm good," Doe said keeping most of his thoughts to himself, "just hold it down and watch your back out there."

"Already, hundred." Pain said before hanging up the phone. He grabbed his keys off the table, then stopped in the kitchen to grab a coke from the fridge and a bag of chips. He walked out the door and got in his Crown Vic. He pulled out his phone and called Nine Milli as he started his car.

"What's the word cuz," Pain said when he answered, "ya'll get Ma Williams to the house"?

"Yeah, we did, Nine Milli said, "sitting over here now smoking a blunt on the porch while she chopping it up with Faba in the crib," Nine Milli said.

"Aight," Pain responded, "step away from the porch so I can put you up on game," Pain told him.

"Ok, give me a few minutes and I will hit your line." He hung up and walked back into the house seeing Faba sitting at the bottom of the stairs with Ma Williams in the kitchen. When Faba looked up and seen Nine Milli he walked over motioning for him to step back outside as they walked passed the porch out to the driveway.

"Aye big bro," Nine Milli said once they were out of earshot, "I gotta go make a run and I will be back in a few."

"Nigga you know what time it is," Faba said softly, "we at war nigga so nobody moves alone!"

"Mane listen," Nine said pulling out his gun, "I'm just running to the store down the street so I can hit Pain back and get some Little Debbie's."

"Snack cake eating ass nigga," Faba said laughing, "how the fuck you got the munchies at a time like this?"

"Cause mary don't give a fuck about beef and war," Nine laughed too, "she gonna make sure a nigga happy, sleepy and hungry."

"You got a hell of a point, just hurry your ass up and get the fuck back here," Faba agreed.

Nine got in his car and started it. "You want something from the store?"

"You know what," Faba smiled, "get me some skittles.

"And you wanna talk shit to me, fucking skittles." Nine said laughing. He drove out the driveway as Faba went back into the house. He pulled out his phone to hit Pain, but he didn't answer so he put his phone in the passenger seat, then turned into the 7-11 parking lot.

He grabbed his gun and made sure it was loaded before he got out of the car and walked to the door holding it open for a few ladies. Entering behind them, he headed to the candy aisle first.

He grabbed a few items and was making a big gulp when he noticed a woman on his left looking at him. He bounced his head at her and then continued making his drink.

She walked up behind him quietly not making a sound before he felt the gun stuck to his side. Nine turned his face looking intensely at Lucy as she stood behind him.

"You must be out of your rabbit ass mind. Get that little shit the fuck off me." She started to put her gun down when Netta walked up to his other side smiling as she put her gun on him looking him in his eyes.

"See I knew Lucy would fall for your soft ass eyes, but you should also know I don't give a fuck." Netta said laughing.

Nine Milli didn't flinch as he picked up his drink. "Man, this is not the day to be playing with me. So, tell me what the fuck ya'll want so I can go pay for my damn Debbie's."

"Shit, we want the bounty on your head," Lucy said pushing him towards the door, "nigga that's a hundred fucking racks."

"Man, I smoke that in a week. What the fuck a hundred racks gonna do for you?"

"See, you thinking way too small," Netta said going out the door, "you gonna give up the stash and the bank to make it all worth it baby."

"So, you bitches have lost your damn mind," Nine said as they pushed him in the truck, "what makes you think I'm gonna tell you anything?"

Netta rubbed a blade across his face. "I wonder how many cuts it's gonna take before you talk, cause baby they all talk at some point."

"Oh, so we playing the cutting game," Nine said looking at the blade, "you must not know who the fuck I am?"

"Oh, I know exactly who you are," Netta said as she cuffed his hands together, "let's get to the warehouse, Lucy."

"Bro, did you see that shit?" Tim said as he got back in the car, "I swear that was that nigga Nine Milli."

"Shit, if it wasn't, that nigga got a fucking twin," Marcus said laughing, "but it look like them chicks had guns on the nigga."

Tim started the car, "I seen that, plus he didn't look too happy getting in the back of that truck."

"Hold up bro," Marcus said without taking his eyes off the truck, "let's go make sure that nigga straight." Marcus told him.

Tim looked as Marcus, grabbed guns from the backseat and handed him one but as soon as they got ready to get out, the truck started pulling off. Tim tapped Marcus and motioned for him to close his door as he put the car in drive and followed them out of the parking lot.

"Oh, we following them?" Marcus said loading another clip, "this may turn into some fun."

"Man, bro it could be some threesome shit for all I know," Tim said laughing, "but I'll feel better knowing than thinking."

Marcus sat his gun on the floor, "I can dig it, don't be following too close with your heavy foot ass."

"Shut your ass up," Tim laughed, "I know how to fucking tail someone."

Ma Williams came out of the kitchen and sat in the living room leaning to pick up a photo album before she sat back on the couch. She opened it and tears instantly ran down her face as she saw a baby picture of Tony and Yetta in a pool.

Losing children is one of the hardest things a parent can go through, and she knew she was no different. Tony dying hit her hard on this day but not knowing if Yetta was alive or dead was making things even worse. Not being able to hold her and tell her that he's gone crushed her.

She continued to flip through the pages letting her mind enjoy the memories before she put the album down and picked up her phone to dial Gripp. He didn't answer so she got up and went back to the kitchen.

Her phone started ringing as she made a glass of wine, so she took it to the table and seen it was Gripp. "How are you Gripp," Ma Williams said when she answered, "how are things in Houston"?

"Hey Ma," Gripp replied, "things are slow we just got here not too long ago."

"Do you have a plan," Ma Williams asked, "or you just gonna set everything on fire"?

Gripp laughed at her question. "I ain't starting no fires, but I do plan to find them before the sun sets tomorrow."

"Well do what you have to do but I have some news for you before I let you go."

"What is it Ma Williams," Gripp said hearing the change in her voice, "why your tone change like that"?

"My son isn't doing well, the injuries may be too much for him this time." Ma Williams fought back tears.

"Wait a damn minute," Gripp said squeezing the phone, "you mean to tell me Tony might die?"

"I know it hurts you just as much as it does me," Ma Williams said finally releasing the tears, "but I'm not telling you this to bring out anger."

"I know you not Ma," Gripp said calming down, "you telling me so that I would hear it from you and not the streets."

"That's one reason," Ma Williams said with a small smile, "but also because no one else in the crew would have had the nuts to tell you or Kesha."

"Kesha..." Gripp said quietly, "I'm gonna kill these niggas either way but if they touch my baby girl the torture will never end."

"You gonna find them in time. Have you heard from Black because he should've made it there by now?" Ma Williams responded.

"Now you know Black as well as I do," Gripp said laughing, "I won't hear from him until he pops up and taps my shoulder." They both had a good laugh as Faba came back in the room motioning his hand. She put Gripp on hold and held down her phone.

"Yes Faba," she said looking up, "what is it?"

"We got the driver of the van," Faba said, "they caught him at the scrap yard dumping it."

Ma Williams stood quickly, "Where is he?" she said getting up, "Take me to that bitch right now?"

"Yes ma'am," Faba said turning around, "I'll go get the car."

She brought her attention back to the phone, "Hello, sorry Gripp but something has come up and I have to call you back."

"Everything ok?" Gripp asked, "You're breathing fast."

"Oh, I'm just putting on my shoes," Ma Williams said laughing, "you know I'm an old lady."

"Alright, call me later." Gripp said before ending the call.

She hung up as she walked out the door to see Faba pulling the car around the driveway, she walked down the stairs and stopped until he held the door for her to get in. "Where is Nine and Doug D?" she asked, "I know they were here earlier."

"Nine went to the store," Faba said, "and Doug D went back to the hospital to make sure Tony's arrangements were in order, but I will text them both in a few."

"Ok," Ma Williams said as he closed the door, "now take me to the pool hall." Faba got in and they left the house and headed to the pool hall. Ma Williams looked at the time as they rode the streets.

Lucy pulled over in the parking lot of an abandoned warehouse and turned off the truck. She grabbed her gun putting it on Nine Milli as they opened the doors and got out.

"Get the fuck out," Netta said pulling on Nine Milli's arm, "I'm not gonna say it twice."

"Damn bitch," Nine Milli said falling out the truck, "you ain't gotta be so ruff with a nigga, you mean ass bitch."

"Nigga shut the fuck up and get your stupid ass in the warehouse," Netta said kicking him. They started walking inside as Tim parked the car across the street. Him and Marcus looked around before they saw them walking in.

"You see that shit," Tim said pointing, "this shit definitely ain't no fucking threesome."

Marcus laughed as they both put new clips in and cocked them before they looked at each other and smiled as they made their way to the warehouse. When they got close, Tim went to the left as Marcus went to the right and found a window open. He stopped and waved at Tim then pointed when he saw Nine Milli walk into an office.

"Sit your ass down in that chair, Netta said, "and put your fucking hands behind your back." When Nine sat down, Netta zip tied his hands and feet and put tape around his mouth then she looked at Lucy motioning her over to the other side of the room.

"Since we killing him anyway," Netta said lighting a blunt, "let's find out where his bag at."

"This nigga ain't about to talk about that bag, let's just shoot his ass and get the fuck out this city," Lucy laughed.

"We will kill the nigga, Lucy," Netta said looking at him, "after we find that fucking stash."

"What makes you think this nigga gonna tell us anything? Cause in case you forgot that nigga a soldier." Lucy asked looking confused.

"Bitch it's simple," Netta said looking up, "because we gonna beat and torture this nigga until he do."

"Ya'll really on this kidnapping shit," Nine Milli said laughing, "or is this a sexy way to say ya'll wanna fuck?" "OUCH!" Nine screamed as Lucy slapped his face then stood over him mugging before she slapped him again.

"You need to watch your fucking mouth," Lucy said rubbing her hand, "I can slap you all got damn day."

"Yeah, you could," Nine Milli said smiling, "but them bitch ass slaps don't hurt me." Lucy laughed then slapped him again as Netta was looking through a toolbox when Nine looked up and smiled hard at Lucy.

"What the fuck is so funny, you lame ass nigga." She raised her hand again motioning towards his face but was caught mid swing, so she turned around as Nine Milli continued to laugh at Tim holding her arm. She tried to yell but he put his hand over her mouth.

"Don't trip," Nine said turning his head, "I got you. Aye Netta, she need you."

"Why the fuck you still talking?" Netta said as she turned around, "she ain't…"

She stopped mid-sentence when she saw Marcus's gun pointed at her face. He grabbed her arm and pushed her beside Lucy before he cut the zip ties from Nine's hands. Nine Milli got up and stretched before he spoke a word.

"Oh my, have the tables fucking turned," Nine said looking at Lucy, "so you wanna repeat that last statement?"

"Fuck you bitch ass nigga, do what the fuck you gonna do without all that noise." Netta said spitting in his face.

"Man let them hoes go, so we can get the fuck out of here." Nine Milli waved his hands.

"Let them go?" Tim said looking at Nine Milli. "Why in the fuck would we do that?"

"Because my nigga," Nine said rubbing his face, "them slaps didn't do shit but turn me on plus leaving them alive lets people think I'm dead."

"Bro what if they come back at you for this bounty, Marcus said still holding his gun on Netta, "we may not be around the next time to save your ass."

"Oh, they ain't coming back," Nine said smiling, "because if they do my people will go see they people and I know they don't want that."

He looked at them both in their eyes and could tell they knew exactly what family he was talking about.

"We ain't coming at you, we gonna head home from here," Lucy said stepping back slowly.

"Now that sounds like a good idea," Nine Milli said tapping Tim, "go ahead and drop that shit." Tim dropped his gun as they watched them walk out the door. Nine Milli made a noise as the door closed.

"Ya'll see all that ass on them chicks? Way too fucking thick to be killers." Nine Milli said laughing.

"You ain't lying," Tim said shaking his head, "cause that girl Netta bad as fuck."

"I'm gonna hit that," Marcus said as they all laughed, "as soon as I get back to the Bluff."

"Nigga you ain't hitting shit, let's get the fuck out of here," Nine Milli told him.

They walked outside to the car and got in before Nine Milli felt his pocket and noticed his phone was missing. He thought for a second and remembered Lucy took it out of his pocket when they went into the warehouse. He shook his head as Tim drove off headed back to the city.

Chapter 9

"Open one," the guard said as they walked through, "close one."

Jermaine jumped when the gate shut behind him. He peeked inside the other cells as they made their way to his box. The guard stopped and Jermaine took a deep breath looking at the silver toilet before noticing the guy inside the cell.

"Get to moving, make yourself at home," The guard said as he shoved him inside.

"Make myself at home? Whatever you say asshole." Jermaine said looking at him sideways. He walked in and put his stuff on the top bunk then started making his bed when three men walked in. One of them tapped his shoulder.

"What's up fresh meat?" Tre eyed him from head to toe and put his arm around his shoulder. "What you in for?"

"Why the fuck you putting your hands on me?" Jermaine said pushing his arm away, "Your mama didn't teach you to keep your hands to yourself?"

"Oh, I see we got a smart ass, I like it when they think they tough," Mike stepped in front of Tre. Mike moved fast grabbing Jermaine, shoving him into the wall before he pushed him down on the toilet and punched him in the face.

"I know you in here for ratting, we bout to show you what we do to snitches," Don said grabbing his neck.

"Nigga I ain't no snitch. Fuck you." Jermaine said pushing his hand. He spat in Don's face before Tre grabbed him punching his face again. Don pulled him off the toilet and reached back to punch him but stopped when he heard Cain speak.

"You little niggas obviously done lost ya'll damn minds. Take your fucking hands off that nigga." Cain said sitting up. Don looked at Cain hard before he let go of Jermaine then slowly started to leave the cell until Cain jumped off his bunk and looked at Jermaine.

"Go make your fucking bed, so I can deal with these niggas." Cain demanded.

"Cain Locc?" Tre said putting up his hands. "You really vouching for this rat?"

"How about you watch your fucking mouth and do what the fuck I tell you to do?" Cain spoke without raising his voice.

"And what the fuck is that? What the fuck is it you would like us to fucking do?" Don looked Cain in the eyes and matched his tone.

"Well for one keep your fucking hands off this nigga, and let everyone in here know that shit," Cain said pointing at Jermaine.

"Alright," Mike said looking at the ground, "Is that it?"

"Naw it ain't, now get your bitch ass the fuck out my crib." Cain moved in their direction.

They moved fast running out the cell as Cain grabbed a pack of Ramen, some crackers, and a bowl. He filled the bowl with water then reached under his pillow and got a phone and tossed it to Jermaine before going back to his food.

"You need to make a call," he said looking at his food, "the nigga is expecting you."

"Who is expecting me?" Jermaine said looking at the number, "don't nobody know I'm here." He pressed send then put the phone to his ear as it started ringing. He watched Cain make his food and it made him wonder how long he was going to be in here and what exactly they were charging him with.

"Jermaine?" Mac said when he answered, "how you holding up in there?"

"Started off a little rocky…" He rubbed his neck before finishing, "but things are calming down."

"That's good," Mac said breathing hard, "we working on getting you out of there as soon as possible."

"We?" Jermaine asked surprised, "who else know I'm in here?"

"Just me and the girls," Mac responded

"What exactly are they charging me with? Jermaine asked, "no one told me anything."

"Well as of now they are charging you with accessory to murder and possession of a controlled substance with the intent to distribute."

"Oh wow," Jermaine said laughing, "they really reaching."

"That's what they do," Mac laughed, "just keep your head up and let's see what the judge says in the morning."

"Ok, anything else?" He replied with a lighter tone.

"Yeah," Mac said, "Your cellmate Cain is your protection so if he tells you to move you move."

"My protection? Why do I need protecting?" Jermaine said confused.

"Because you have a job to do," Mac answered, "and he will make sure you get it done."

"Alright, I hear you talking."

"Good, I will see you in court." Mac ended the call. Jermaine looked at the phone for a minute after Mac hung up before handing it back to Cain. He sat back and laid on his bunk as Cain turned around.

"So, you ratted on Gripp for going after Big Ben," Cain said stirring his soup, "or did you keep your fucking mouth shut?"

"I'm in with your ass ain't I? Which means I didn't say shit." Jermaine responded with an attitude.

"Naw it don't," Cain said looking at him, "you could've talked and they just put you here till they verify your story."

"Well, I ain't got no story," Jermaine said, "I'm just a poet with a boring life."

"Poet huh," Cain said handing him a bowl, well let me hear something."

Gripp woke up the next morning with a lot on his mind. Not knowing what his next move would be as he sat on the end of the bed. He reached for his phone and saw he had two missed calls from Ma Williams. He sat the phone back on the bed and went to the bathroom.

When he came out, he heard a knock on the door, so he grabbed his gun as he saw Nick through the peephole before he opened it.

"What's good Gripp?" Nick said stepping into the room. "You alright this morning?"

"I'm just ready to find my girls," Gripp said putting on his shoes, "where is Doe?"

"I thought he was in here with you," Nick scanned the room, "he wasn't in his room."

"Where the hell could he be? I will call him after I call Ma Williams back but first let's get the fuck out of here," Gripp said picking up his phone. They got on the elevator as Gripp unlocked his phone and dialed Ma Williams. She answered as they were exiting.

"Good morning Gripp," Ma Williams said, "how are things in Houston?"

"Morning Ma, things are about to heat up. We're leaving the hotel as soon as we find Doe."

"Doe is with Black," Ma Williams responded, "he picked him up last night."

"Why the fuck is Doe with Black?" Gripp said, "And why would he leave without telling us?"

"Oh, I see no one has called you," Ma Williams said, guess they feel you need to hear it from me?"

"Hear what?" Gripp asked intrigued, "Cause no one called me."

"Tony died at the hospital..." Ma Williams spoke slowly, "the damage was too much this time."

"What you mean Tony died?" Gripp said, "I thought he was just critical?"

"Yes, and they tried for hours but in the end, he didn't make it."

"Son of a bitch, I'm going to kill all these niggas."

"Before you do," Ma Williams said stopping him, "there are a few other things I must tell you."

"So, there is more," Gripp said as he and Nick walked to the car, "lay it on me."

"Jermaine is in lockup and Nine was taken but the Bakers got to him before the ladies could do any real damage."

"Well, that's not all bad news," Gripp said relieved, I thought you were gonna say someone else was dead."

"Well..." she hesitated, "one of the girls was murdered by Big Ben while Pain was on video chat."

"Are you telling me that one of my girls is dead?" Gripp stopped in the middle of the parking lot. "Is that what you saying, Ma Williams."

"I'm sorry Gripp," Ma responded, "but it's best if you know everything that's going on."

"So, who got killed?" Gripp asked holding his breath, "and where is the body?"

"It was Mastarpiece" Ma Williams said with tears, "and her body is somewhere with Nick's right hand Smooth."

"Smooth?" Gripp said looking at Nick, "So, Big Ben just killing everyone?"

"I think he was trying to prove he was in control," apparently Smooth got in his way."

"That's because the nigga a soldier," Gripp said giving props, "I will call you later on today."

"Be careful Gripp," Ma Williams said worried, "I want you all home in one piece."

"Gone," Gripp said hanging up the phone as he walked over to the car. He stood and looked at Nick for a minute before he spoke.

"Big Ben killed your right hand," Gripp said unlocking the door, "killed Mastarpiece too."

"That fat lumpy piece of shit," Nick said as anger took over, "man let's hurry up and find that bitch."

"You read my mind," Gripp said getting in, "we going to start with the safe house in stop six cause we will know if they been there or not yet."

"Cool," Nick said, "what we doing about Doe?"

"That nigga with Black," Gripp said, "he must've heard about Tony last night and dipped."

"What about Tony," Nick asked confused, "that nigga aight ain't he"?

"Naw, he died from the gunshot wounds," Gripp responded, "they tried but couldn't save him."

"Gotttt damn," I know Yetta and Kesha going to be pissed the fuck off behind this shit." Nick said shaking his head.

"Ain't nobody as pissed as Doe is right now, Gripp said smiling, "I just hope the nigga leave some bodies for us."

"Right," Nick agreed putting on his seat belt, "cause I still owe that nigga Howard from back in the day and would love to put a bullet in his head."

Gripp drove out of the parking lot moving through the streets of Houston as he pulled out his phone to dial Doe but didn't get an answer so he sent a 911 text before setting it down.

"There goes the exit right there," Nick said pointing, "it should get us to the block."

Gripp got off and stopped at a red light pulling out a cigar as they waited for it to turn green. Nick looked in the mirror and saw the van first, so he reacted fast reaching for the guns in the backseat.

"What's the deal, Nick," Gripp asked as he gave him a look, "you checking the guns?"

"Oh, I'm about to check them alright," Nick said cocking a 45 before handing it to Gripp, "we got company behind us."

"Which one," Gripp said looking in his mirror, "blue or black?"

"It's the black one," Nick said, "it's been on us since we left the hotel."

They both sat back with guns in their lap till the light turned green then Gripp pressed the gas lightly slowly going through the light before he hit it hard speeding through the streets.

The van was right on their ass until it pulled beside them. The side door opened and two men with AR-15 rifles started shooting up the car. Gripp hit the brakes hard watching them fly by. Nick jumped out of the car and started firing at the van as Gripp made his way to the back of the car. The men moved around the van and positioned themselves before they started firing back bullets that hit every part of the car.

Gripp tapped Nick and pointed at the building next to them. Nick nodded as they both got up shooting and running towards the building. As they entered, Nick turned to shoot again but was stopped by the bullet hitting his chest. He fell to the ground and took a deep breath before he saw Gripp come out with two guns shooting anything moving.

He grabbed Nick and dragged him into the building before picking him up and carrying him into an office. Sitting him down on the desk he could feel the vest Nick had on.

"Your dumb ass wore a vest, Gripp said laughing, about time you used your big ass head for something."

"You aint lying, Nick said laughing, shit still hurts like a bitch."

"Yeah, I know Gripp said helping him up, I think I hit a couple of them but we gonna wait here till the coast is clear to leave."

"Wait here," Nick said standing all the way up, cause we are sitting ducks in here Gripp."

"Naw we ain't, Gripp said, they going to think it's a trap so they ain't coming in here."

"So, what's the plan on getting the fuck out of here, Nick asked confused, cause I don't trust walking out that door."

"I don't either, Gripp said pulling out his phone, so I'm going to call Carlos and have him come get us."

"I know you ain't talking about Buie," Nick said quickly, cause I thought he got out the game years ago."

"He is out the game," Gripp said, but the gangster in him never dies so he always comes thru when I call."

"He always been a solid nigga," Nick said, and smart as fuck."

"Yeah, he was the best money man in the game," Gripp said, "I hated to lose the connect who could wash a million dollars with ease."

"Well hit him up," Nick said rubbing his chest, "I'm going to take a peek at what's going on outside."

"Aight," Gripp said standing up, here take this shotgun just in case."

Nick grabbed the shotgun and headed out of the office as Gripp dialed Carlos but he didn't answer so Gripp sent a text letting him know it was him calling. A few seconds later the phone rang. "Gripp the super Crip, Carlos said when he answered, to what do I owe the pleasure of this call?"

"What's going on Buie," Gripp said responding, "I'm calling because I need a favor bro."

"A favor," Carlos asked confused, "now you know I'm out the game plus I don't even talk to the old connects since I moved to Houston."

"Naw, not that type of favor," Gripp laughed, "we out here in Houston and ran into a little trouble so we need a lift."

"What the hell you doing in Houston," Carlos said grabbing his keys, "do I need my pistol?"

"Yeah, you better bring it," Gripp said, "and I will fill you in once we're in the car."

"Ok bet," Carlos said getting in the car, "send me your location and I'm on my way."

"That's a bet," Gripp said, "I'm gonna shoot it to you now."

"Already," Carlos said, "be there in two shakes of a lion's tail."

"Gone," Gripp responded as he hung up the phone then grabbed his gun and headed out the office to join Nick at the door.

"What's going on," Gripp asked once he was beside him, "them bitches left yet?"

"Yeah," Nick said, "they played around for a minute then searched the car before they left."

"Searched the car," Gripp asked with an attitude, "did those bitches take my Glocks?"

"Hell, yeah they did," Nick said laughing, "and my 1911."

"Mother Fuckers, well Carlos is on his way so once we get in another car, we gonna deal with them."

"Already," Nick said pulling out a blunt, "you got a light?"

Doe and Black pulled into the Quik Trip outside the neighborhood. Knowing the type of environment they were in made them move with caution. Black pulled out his phone and sent a text as Doe went into the store to grab drinks. When he came back out he could see an SUV pull in behind Black and park so he pulled out his gun and moved fast reaching the truck as the door opened to a guy with dreads. He put the gun directly between his eyes.

"Did you think a light-skinned nigga would be the death of you today? Or would you like the black ass nigga over there to do it?"

"Got damn bro," Fresh said looking as his uncle walked up, "you niggas ain't hospitable at all huh Uncle Black?"

"Calm down Doe," Black said laughing, that's my nephew Fresh from Stop Six."

"Nigga better make hisself known next time," Doe put away his gun. "Cause I normally shoot first, ask questions later."

"I sure am glad you chose today to ask first," Fresh said relieved, "but fuck all that."

"So, nephew," Black said shaking his hand, "what's been going on in the hood today?"

"Three of Big Ben people holed up at that nigga Joe crib," Fresh said pointing down the street, "and they all strapped up."

"You talking about the house in the cul-de-sac," Black asked, "with the garden?"

"That's the one and I got a bitch on the inside with them right now so you can move on them when you ready unc."

"Damn nephew," Black said hugging his head, "you have learned a lot from me."

"You know me, uncle Black, you always taught me to pay attention to my surroundings and plus I been here forever so I know everything happening in these streets."

"Aight Fresh," Doe said popping the trunk, "your muscle in place?"

"Everyone in place and ready to set this shit off," Fresh said pulling out his phone, "as soon as they get the green light."

Alright", Black said grabbing guns, "let them know it's time."

"Got you unc, give me one sec."

"Did this nigga say give him a sec," Doe said laughing, "damn kids kill me."

"Aye Dante, Fresh said into the phone, "it's going down like the bottom of shoes."

He hung up as Doe continued to get ready.

"Let's go get these bitches." Doe said

They all got in Fresh's SUV and headed down the street to Stop Six noticing the closer they got to the house the more niggas came outside. Fresh parked at the house next door then texted Shavonn.

Fresh: How many in there?

Shavonn: It's 4. 3 in the front room and one in the back.

Fresh: Where your girls at?

Shavonn: Robyn and Monet in the kitchen with me. Yolanda in the back with Joe.

Fresh: Alright. Head to the back door and get the fuck out of there. We coming in.

Shavonn: What about Yolanda?

Fresh: I'll make sure she good. Now go.

"Alright, we good," Fresh turned his attention back to the team, "we going in through the back."

They got of out the SUV and were headed towards the backyard when Fresh saw the girls, he pushed them out the gate before he closed it then waved to the men in the front and they all started moving.

Black went in first with Doe following him. Once they were in the kitchen, they could see Lamar, Ron and Nell sitting in the living room watching tv. Doe moved slowly walking through the kitchen as Fresh followed him into the living room. He put the tip of his gun to the back of Lamar's head.

"What the fuck?!" Lamar said as he turned to the barrel of Doe's gun. Ron turned when he heard Lamar and tried to reach for his gun until he heard Fresh cock the shotgun. Nell was about to make a move until he looked up and saw Black standing in the door, so he sat back down as Black walked over and opened the front door.

"We going upstairs," Black said pointing at Doe, yall tie these bitches up."

"No problem," Dante said pulling out zip ties, "then what Gripp?"

"Fresh," Gripp answered, "pull the truck up and put they ass in the back."

"All of them unc," Fresh asked looking around the room, "you sure they gone fit?"

"One way or another they will," Black said laughing, "I don't give a fuck if they comfortable or not. Black turned and followed Doe as he moved up the stairs, tiptoeing to the back room. Black put his ear to the door and could hear Yolanda moaning so he nodded at Doe while twisting the door knob slowly until it opened. He walked in holding the door as Doe moved past him towards the bed.

Doe could see Yolanda holding Joe's head between her legs as he walked up slowly pushing Joe's head deeper with his gun. Yolanda looked up and screamed before Joe could get the blanket over his head. Doe put his finger to her lips and she got quiet as Joe rolled off the bed.

"What the fuck is this shit," Joe said leaning against the dresser, "you know who the fuck I am, nigga?"

"I know exactly who you are," Black said walking in and turning on the light, now put some fucking clothes on." Joe didn't move at the sight of Black standing in his room because if he didn't know shit else about him, he knew Black didn't make house calls.

"Nigga did you hear what the fuck he just said!?" Doe yelled grabbing a pair of pants, "put on some got damn clothes!"

"You can get dressed too, then you can get out of here," Black said to Yolanda. She didn't say a word as she grabbed her clothes and ran out the door before even putting them on.

"Say, man," Joe said standing up, "I don't know why ya'll in my house, but somebody need to start doing some explaining?"

"Nigga we ain't gotta explain shit to your bitch ass, now get your punk ass the fuck downstairs," Doe said walking up and pushing Joe out the room.

Joe started moving as Doe walked behind them. He peaked downstairs once they were close enough and saw that the living room was empty. When he was two steps from the bottom, he took off running out of the door. "Stupid ass nigga," Doe yelled coming down the steps, "aye yo Fresh!"

Fresh turned and saw Joe coming out the door, so he grabbed his gun and fired a shot that hit Joe in the leg. Joe instantly fell to the ground as Doe walked over laughing and stood in front of him. "See what all that extra shit get you," Doe said looking at him, a bullet in the fucking leg."

"Man do what the fuck you gonna do," Joe yelled spitting on the ground, "I'm really tired of hearing your raggedy ass voice!"

"Oh yeah," Doe said reaching in his pocket, "well let's fucking take care of that problem now." He smiled as he grabbed Joe by his beard with one hand and released the blade of the knife with the other. He reached down and cut off Joe's right ear then let his face fall to the ground. He was still screaming when Black walked out the door.

"Where your boss got my Goddaughter," Black asked nicely, "and I'm only gonna ask you once."

"The nigga got a safe house by the airport," Joe said holding his ear, "I will take you there if you get this nigga to back the fuck up."

"Naw, he can't do that," Doe said pulling out his nine, "but don't trip we'll find it." He shot Joe in the head twice then put his gun back in his waist as he looked up at Fresh standing beside him in silence. "That's for Tony you bitch ass nigga, Doe said spitting on his face, hope your ass already burning."

"Now why in the fuck would you kill the nigga," Fresh said looking at Doe, "when he was gonna take us to the safehouse?"

"Two reasons my guy," Doe said tapping his shoulder, "we still got three bitches that I bet gonna tell us quickly."

"I get that part, but what's the second?"

"This nigga fucked over Tony a few years back before his ass ran to Houston," Doe said looking around, "so since Tony ain't here I handled it for him."

"Oh shit," Black said looking at the guys coming out of the house, "we need to get the fuck out of here."

"You right unc," Fresh said, "let's ride."

They all got in the truck as the guys got closer to the house. When Fresh pulled off, they saw Joe's body lying on the ground, so they started shooting at them. An SUV pulled up and the niggas got in and started chasing them. One of the guys stood out the sunroof emptying clips at Fresh's truck.

"Bitch ass niggas," Doe yelled as he shot at the SUV behind them, "you fucking with the right one today!"

Boom, Boom, Boom was all you heard in the hood of stop six as niggas came from every corner with guns shooting at them so Fresh made a quick left and got on the highway as Doe reloaded. Black reached back and grabbed an AR-15 from the bag in the back seat then handed it to Doe.

"Now that's what the fuck I'm talking about," Doe said cocking the gun, "you should've been gave me this!"

Doe turned around and fired continuously at the SUV behind them hitting it with every bullet till it finally started spinning out of control hitting a guard rail before catching on fire. Doe laughed as he sat back down in the seat and handed the AR-15 back to Black.

"Awe fuck," Doe said looking in the very back, "ain't this bout a bitch."

"What's up Doe?" Black said turning around, "oh damn." Both Nell and Ron had multiple bullet holes including headshots. Lamar was still breathing but really fucked up. Doe sat back and lit a blunt as Fresh made his way thru the streets. "Guess I should've let Joe take us to the house, instead of blowing his brains out."

"It wouldn't matter anyway," Black said, "he would've bled out from the ear anyway."

"You think so, I only cut off one ear," Doe said as he turned his head.

"Naw nigga, Fresh said laughing hard, "you cut off part of his face so he definitely would of bled out by now."

"Damn, I wish I would of knew that shit before I shot him," Doe said.

"Why you say that? Either way he's dead." Black asked.

"After what that bitch ass nigga did to Tony bro, a very slow death would have been a lot better," Doe said closing his eyes.

"Damn Doe, you a cold-blooded asshole," Fresh said looking in the mirror.

"You better know it," Doe laughed, "let's hurry up and get to the warehouse before these niggas start smelling."

"I got you bro, we about 10 minutes away"

"Bet and I'm hungry as shit," Doe told Fresh.

Big Ben was sitting in the living room of the safe house eating some chips when his phone started ringing. He looked at it and saw it was Wesley from stop six and sat it back down and continued to watch his show. A few minutes later James came into the living room and stood beside the couch.

"Boss," James held a phone in his view of the TV, "Wesley on the phone and he say it's important."

"Can't you see I'm watching the fucking game," Big Ben said, "what the fuck does the nigga want?"

"I don't fucking know," James said with an attitude, "he asked for you, not me."

Big Ben turned his head and looked up at James. He laughed as he sat his chips on the table and stood up.

"You got balls boy, Big Ben said grabbing the phone, "big balls."

"Whatever, we in the kitchen." He left the room before Ben could respond.

Big Ben sat back down and put the phone to his ear.

"Why the hell you calling," Big Ben yelled in the phone, "interrupting my game and shit."

"Sorry about that boss," Wesley responded, "but we got a problem."

"Is it really that important that you have to interrupt me while I'm watching the game," Big Ben asked, well is it?"

"Joe is…dead," Wesley hesitated, "Doe killed him a few hours ago."

"What the fuck you mean Joe's dead? So, you saying Gripp is fucking in Houston?"

"Naw, boss, it was Doe and Black and they got a couple of our guys too."

"Fuck," Big Ben said getting up, "where they at now?"

"I don't know boss," Wesley answered, "but we shot the truck up pretty good so they probably laying low somewhere."

"Alright, clean that shit up and gather a few guys cause it's time to go hunting." Big Ben walked to the kitchen and looked at his men sitting at the table then looked at the door to the basement noticing it had been left open. "Which one of you went down there, and for what reason?"

"The women needed water," James said looking at him, "so I took some down there."

"And who told you to fucking be concerned with what they need," Big Ben asked, "stupid shit."

James continued to look at him wondering if he was serious or not.

"I know you the boss, James said, "but honestly, I couldn't care less because they are not animals bro." Big Ben walked up to James and slapped him out of his chair. He looked at him quickly before he kicked him in the stomach.

"Them big balls of yours gonna get you fucked up, especially if you keep being disobedient." Big Ben said as he stared him down. He turned and walked to the basement door then opened it as the cold air hit him fast. He turned on the light and started walking down the stairs into the space the girls were being held. He flicked the light switch looking at Kesha and Yetta laying on the bed then walked in and closed the door.

"You know under different circumstances this is a sexy ass scene," Big Ben said walking around the bed, "two bitches on a bed tied up."

"Fuck you with some aids pussy, I hope you die fast bitch," Yetta said spitting on the floor.

"See," Big Ben said laughing, "that's why your friend got shot in her face and I guess you want that same fate?"

"Bitch shut the fuck up," Kesha said looking in his eyes, "you not gonna touch me or my fucking sister."

"And how the fuck you figure that, who the fuck gonna stop me."

"Ain't nobody gotta stop you," Kesha said smiling, "don't sit there and act like I don't already know you like dick more than we do."

"Bitch," Big Ben said with anger, "you better watch your fucking mouth."

"Oh, your feelings hurt," Kesha said laughing, "poor little bitch."

"You know what," Big Ben said pacing, "I can't wait to send you to visit your bitch ass boyfriend."

"Send me," Kesha said laughing, "bitch he probably already here waiting to put a bullet through your fucking eye."

"Oh, he is nowhere near a threat to me anymore," Big Ben said laughing, "cause that little bitch is dead."

"You a got damn lie," Kesha said yelling at him, "and I'm gonna be right there when he pull the trigger." Big Ben turned and opened the door before he laughed hard and walked back up the stairs to the kitchen. James finally got off the floor and was standing by the refrigerator.

"Load they ass in the van," Big Ben said looking around when he made it upstairs, "we leaving in a few."

"What's the fucking rush now," James laughed, "thought you wanted to watch the fucking game."

"Black is in town," Big Ben said walking towards his room, "and you know it won't take him long to find us."

"Let me find out you scared of Black," James said smiling, "not badass Big Ben."

"To be honest I never met him, but my father always told me if you know Black is coming for you to run."

He walked into the room and closed the door as James looked at the twins standing by the table. He started to say something, but Harold beat him to the punch.

"Man, I really don't see the point of all this bullshit, we all know Gripp will never pay this nigga."

"Yeah," Howard said, "I know but what the fuck you want me to do, shit you heard the boss."

"Only thing I hear is he don't have a fucking plan," Howard said, "and now Black is coming for these chicks?"

"Bro Black is already here," James said looking at him, "that phone call was Wesley saying Joe got popped and Black did it."

"Oh fuck," Howard said standing up, "if they killed Joe that means they know where we at."

"You right," James said following suit, "we need to get the fuck up out of here."

"Right," Harold said grabbing the keys, "I'll get the van while ya'll go get the girls." They started moving with some pep in their step. Wesley reached down and cut the zip ties from the girl's hands while Howard held the gun, picked them up and put tape on their mouths. He pushed them up the stairs to the kitchen and out the back door towards the van.

As the girls were being loaded into the van, Big Ben was walking out of his room with a bag and a suitcase. He grabbed two guns on his way out the door and got into the van. He looked around before he closed the door.

"Put those bags in the back," Big Ben said to Harold, "and hurry the fuck up."

"OK," Harold said grabbing the bags, "I got it."

After he put the bags in the back and closed the door he walked around and opened the driver's door, looking around as he got in. He pulled off not knowing where they were going. He just kept driving.

Gripp and Nick were passing the airport when his phone rang. He looked at it and saw it was Doe so he answered.

"What up Doe," Gripp said, "where the hell you been?"

"Bro me and Black on the hunt and I just killed that bitch ass nigga Joe."

"Joe?" Gripp said confused, "Who the fuck is that?"

"He talking about Joe that works for Ben," Nick said tapping his shoulder, "the nigga that fucked over Tony back in the day."

"Oh, I remember now," Gripp said laughing, "Tony been wanting that nigga dead for years."

"Well in his honor, it's done, and the nigga said they got the girls at a safe house by the airport," Doe told him.

"Yeah, that's what Nick said," Gripp responded, "we actually passing the airport now."

"Yall already got a location?" Doe asked looking at Black, send that bitch to us."

"Bet, Gripp said, we will get it sent in a few."Gripp noticed a truck when he looked in his mirror as he hung up the phone and grabbed a gun from the back seat. Nick looked at him and without question grabbed one too.

"Which vehicle," Nick said checking the chamber, "car or truck?"

"The blue truck about three cars back," Gripp continued to check the mirror, "it's been following us for a few miles."

"You sure it's not a coincidence," Nick said, "or family?"

"Oh, I'm sure, Gripp told him while making a left, "the driver wearing a ski mask."

"Bet," Nick said getting in the back seat, "hit a back road."

Gripp turned right on Macarthur then pulled into a parking garage. He drove to the second level and slowed down as Nick jumped out of the car and hid behind an SUV then he continued to drive.

The truck hit the corner driving slow as it made its way through the garage. It continued driving until it came to the car parked in the curve. The doors opened and three men got out with AR-15 rifles. Two went towards the car while the other walked towards the curve.

Nick moved to the front of the SUV with his gun pointed at the two men by the car. He looked up and saw Gripp standing in the curve, so he moved closer before firing four shots, hitting both men. The third gunman turned around as their bodies fell to the ground. He saw Nick and started to pull the trigger when he felt a bullet hit his shoulder. He dropped his gun before he turned and saw Gripp standing behind him.

"Who sent you and how many more are coming?"

"Big Ben sent us," he said looking at Gripp, "it's a million bounty on you and half a million for any of your top crew."

"Well damn I'm only worth a million dollars," Gripp said looking at Nick, "guess I gotta do better."

"I guess so," Nick laughed, "or Big Ben ain't got it like we think."

"What you think," Gripp said pointing his gun at the gunman, "you think Big Ben got it like that?"

"I'm just in it for the money," he said looking at Gripp, "I could care less what he got or don't got."

"That's real shit," Nick said walking to the car, "Gripp, please kill this bitch so we can go." Boom! That was the only sound you heard before Gripp walked around and got in the car, started it, then drove off. He paid the ticket then was headed towards the safe house when he pulled out his phone and dialed Pain's number.

"What's good pops?" Pain said when he answered, "Tell me you found them."

"Not yet, Gripp said, "but I need you to get everyone on high alert."

"High alert?" Pain asked, "My sister missing that ain't high enough?"

"It's a bounty on us," Gripp replied, "so people will be coming down from everywhere trying to collect."

"Oh word, how much is the bounty?" Pain laughed at the thought.

"It's a million on me," Gripp laughed too, "but only half on yall."

"Man, I wish someone would come at me for five hundred. I'm gonna kill him for being stupid."

"You sound like this nigga Nick," Gripp said, he just told me to pop one of they asses."

"What you mean," Pain said sitting up, "they already came at you?"

"Yeah," Gripp responded, "three deep but we got the drop on them easily."

"Alright," Pain said pissed off, "time to turn up the heat."

Ma Williams sat at the lake looking at the water. Alex and Richard were standing behind her when they heard Faba's phone ring. He looked at it and stepped away before he answered. "You bold as fuck," Faba said when he answered, "what the fuck you want?"

"I want my fucking money," Big Ben said, "cause you running out of time."

"First off..." Faba started, "how the fuck did you get my number? And second, what the fuck makes you think you getting anything from us bitch?"

"I already killed one of them bitches," Big Ben said, "still need me to prove a point?"

Ma Williams heard him talking so she turned around and could tell from his face who he was talking too. She motioned for Alex to give her a phone then texted Nick and told him to call Wallace to trace the call on Faba's phone.

"You ain't proved shit," Faba said, "plus you will be dead before you get a chance to count that money."

"Nigga please," Big Ben said laughing, "you will never catch me."

Ma William's phone went off with a text saying "got it" so she put it away and got up. She nodded at Faba and walked off.

118

"See you soon nigga," Faba said hanging up.

Nick looked at his phone and seen the text from Ma Williams, so he texted Wallace. He texted back two minutes later with a location. He sent it to Doe before he spoke to Gripp.

"I think we got a lock on where they at," Nick said looking at his phone, "it's only like ten minutes from where we at now."

"You send it to Doe?" Gripp asked turning around the car, "and let him know we headed that way now."

"Bet," Nick said sending the text, "let's get these bitches."

Doe checked his phone and seen the address from Nick. He showed it to Black before putting it in the GPS and seen they were just eight minutes from the location. Black started speeding through the streets blowing through every light before he hit the neighborhood.

Harold was unloading the van when Howard came outside and handed him the phone. "Who is that?" Harold said taking the phone, "cause I know you see I'm busy."

"It's your baby mama," Howard said irritated, calling my fucking phone for you."

"Unload the van," Harold said, "I'll be back."

He walked off and put the phone to his ear. Nick was standing on the side of the house watching when Black pulled in the driveway and parked looking at Harold on the phone.

"Fuck this shit," Doe said swinging his door open, "I'm tired of fucking waiting." He moved fast shooting Harold in the neck as he made his way towards Howard but before he could make it to him gunfire rang out as bullets hit the van and car putting holes all over it. Doe jumped behind a tree and hit the ground.

Howard jumped in the van missing the bullets. He saw Doe running as he grabbed an AR-15 and started shooting out the back door. He held up his hand and the shooting stopped as he got out.

Gripp came out of nowhere shooting at the men on the porch as bullets started ringing again. Howard continued shooting until he made his way in the house. "Fucking kill everybody," He yelled, moving through the house, "I'm going to get Ben." He ran off and up the stairs as the other men moved towards the outside but stopped at the door when they saw the others dead on the porch and only one man still standing.

Black looked on the roof where another gunman stood, so he grabbed a scope and snapped it on his gun then fired shooting hitting him through his own scope.

Once it was quiet again Gripp came out and the five of started walking towards the back porch with Fresh in front. Nick stopped and lit a Newport before he checked his gun.

Fresh walked on the porch looking at the bodies not noticing the men in the doorway. A shot rang out hitting him in the back. Black looked up and ran to him as they all started shooting.

"Big Ben!" Howard yelled down the hall, "We gotta get the fuck out of here right now!"

"What the fuck is going on down there?" Ben said putting on his clothes, "All that fucking noise."

"Are you fucking kidding me?" Howard said irritated, "That's Gripp coming to get what's his and the nigga already killed my brother."

"What you mean?" Big Ben said grabbing his gun, "How the fuck did they find us?"

"I don't fucking know but they did, so it's time to fucking go but I can't fucking find James?"

"James," Big Ben said looking up, "Um I don't know but you should go and find him then meet me in the garage."

"Alright," Howard said looking at him, "But why the hell your voice get high and shit?"

"Really?" Big Ben asked, "That's what you worried about dumbass?"

Howard shook his head and closed the door. Big Ben waited a few seconds before he opened the closet and let James come out.

"You almost got us caught this time Ben," James said still putting on his clothes, "trying to suck my soul out."

"Well, I like the way you feel in my mouth," Big Ben said, "and you had the back of my head."

"I was caught up in that nut," James said kissing Big Ben, "now let's get the fuck out of here." They moved to the door and heard silence, so James opened it seeing Howard standing outside the door. He tapped him on the shoulder and they all went towards the stairs. Gunshots started again so they ran to the garage and got in one of the cars.

"Nigga where the fuck did you come from?" Howard said looking at James, "cause I didn't see you in the room."

"I was in the side room taking a nap," James said looking at him, "he didn't tell you?"

"Naw," Howard said, "the nigga sent me to look for you."

"How about you both shut the fuck up," Big Ben said opening his door, "and go get the fucking girls."

"What," Howard said, "nigga you out your damn mind if you think I'm running back in that house."

"Really," Big Ben said laughing, "you do what the fuck I tell you to do which means get your bitch ass in the fucking house and go get them got damn girls!"

Howard got out with an attitude and went into the house as James started the car. Big Ben watched as he went in and closed the door then he turned and grabbed James by the neck kissing him deeply as he unbuttoned his pants.

"Right now," James said as he pulled back, "in the middle of all this?"

"My word ya'll are hard-headed," Big Ben said, "do what I said damn it." He pushed James down and moaned as he wet his mouth and took him in. His hand controlled the motion as James went to work taking every bit of what Ben had to give.

Gripp and Doe jumped behind the van as Nick kept shooting towards the porch. Black pulled Fresh off the porch and to the side of the house. Nick finally fell back and stood beside Doe as they kept shooting at the house.

The men started coming out shooting towards the van when a bullet went through a window and hit Gripp in the shoulder making him hit the ground as Doe ran over to him. When Nick saw Gripp fall his brain did a flip and he grabbed an extra gun off the ground. He got up and started blasting hitting one guy in the leg and the other one in the chest then ran up and kicked the gun from his hands.

The reflection from the gun hit the corner of his eye. He turned fast firing at the porch hitting the guy with multiple bullets. Looking around he went to check on Gripp.

"Aye," Nick said, "you good?"

"Yeah," Gripp said holding on to Doe, "it went straight through."

"Bet," Nick said walking off, "I'm going in." He walked away as Black picked up Fresh and carried him to the car then watched as Doe helped Gripp in the car and run over to him.

"Let's go," Nick said opening the door, "and shoot anything that moves." They walked in looking around the house. Nick went to the kitchen as Doe made his way to the rooms. Nick looked up and saw Howard creeping through the kitchen.

Nick motioned at Doe as he put up his gun. He shot once hitting Howard in the leg before running up and standing on top of him pointing at his head. "Don't you fucking move," Nick warned, "please try me."

Doe walked over but heard a car running in the garage, so he turned and walked towards the door. When he opened it...

Big Ben pushed James's head hard when he heard the shot. James jumped up and looked behind him just as the door opened. He saw Doe's face peek through, and his eyes got wide. He put the car in drive and hit the gas speeding out the driveway.

Doe saw James's body come up out of nowhere.

"What the fuck", he said as he looked in the car, "is that nigga...?"

Doe heard the car go into gear as he aimed at the driver, so he started shooting at it as it sped out the driveway. He chased it to the end but knew he couldn't catch it, so he turned around and walked back to the house.

Black was parked on the street when he heard the tires screech and the shooting start. He grabbed a gun from Gripp and checked the clip opening his door just in time to see the car speed past them. He jumped back in the car, put it in gear, then hit the gas. "What's up, Gripp asked looking at Black, we leaving them?"

"That's Big Ben in that car," Black said chasing them, "Doe and Nick will figure it out."

He continued chasing them.

Nick kept the gun on Howard as the shooting outside died. Doe walked back in and went to the refrigerator for something to drink. He opened it and grabbed a coke and sat his gun on the counter.

"Big Ben and that other bitch got away," Doe said breathing hard, "I'm too old to be chasing cars."

"Your ass too old to be chasing that coke you drinking too," Nick said laughing, "but I truly understand."

"Fuck you," Doe said laughing, "have you questioned his ass yet because the girls wasn't in the car."

"Really?" Nick said looking back at Howard, "So, since they left you I'm gonna give you one chance to tell me where they at or catch one in the face."

Howard looked up at Doe sipping on the coke then back at Nick. He realized the shit wasn't worth dying for. "If I tell you, can I walk out of here?"

"I tell you what," Nick said putting his gun away. "If you tell me, you can go, and I promise I won't kill you."

Harold took a deep breath before he spoke.

"They in the basement," Howard said pointing, "under that couch in the living room."

Doe looked in the living room at the couch then walked over and kicked it backward till he saw the bare floor. He got on his knees to search for a latch or way to open it but didn't find anything. He turned back to Howard. "I think you're full of shit," Doe said standing up, "it's not a door over here."

Howard sat up and turned around looking at the spot Doe was standing.

"That's because that's the wrong one," Howard pointed and told him, "It's under the bean bag couch." Doe laughed before he walked over and pushed the bean bag couch out the way revealing a door then reached down and pulled it open before he nodded at Nick.

"Get the fuck out of here," Nick said walking over to Doe, "better be gone by the time I get back up here."

Nick and Doe made their way down the basement stairs until they reached the bottom. It was dark with no switch in reachable length, so Doe pulled out his phone and moved it around the room till he saw bodies lying on the bed.

126

He walked over and pulled the sheet from Kesha's head then took a deep breath as he continued to pull until it was on the floor. He looked at Nick and smiled before he leaned down and touched Kesha's face. She jumped not knowing who was touching her. She moved as close to Yetta as she could before he took the blindfold.

She blinked a few times before actually opening her eyes. When she looked up, she screamed and cried at the sight of Doe's face.

Nick walked up and waved at Kesha before he took the blindfold from Yetta's face. She looked up at Nick and for a second, she thought she was dreaming until she looked over at Doe cutting Kesha from the bed. "Am I dreaming, Yetta asked looking at Kesha, "or are we really being saved?"

"Hey," Nick said touching her face, "we just killed like a hundred niggas to find you so we can take you home."

"Hey Nick and thank you." Yetta said smiling.

"Girl please," Nick said laughing, "let me get you untied."

Kesha jumped up and hugged Doe once he got her loose. Yetta did the same to Nick but wouldn't let his neck go so he reached down and picked her up. Doe pulled a gun from his waist and handed it to Kesha. She checked the chamber and got up off the bed.

"Aight," Doe said pointing his phone towards the stairs, "let's get up out of here."

"You just don't know how long I been waiting to hear that," Kesha said following behind Doe, "I'm so ready."

Doe led as they made their way up the stairs. Getting low he slowly opened the door and went into the living room scanning all around before he reached down and helped Kesha up. She walked through the house while Doe helped get Yetta up.

Nick made it up and closed the door before turning around. Yetta walked into a room and looked in the dresser for something to put on her feet. She found some socks and grabbed a pair for Kesha.

Kesha jumped as the socks hit her face when Yetta tossed them to her. She turned and seen Yetta laughing so she smiled too. Nick walked to the back door and looked outside to make sure no one was waiting for them. Doe went to the garage then walked to the end of the driveway and looked down the street.

"I wonder where the hell Black at," Doe said looking around, "I thought he would be parked right here."

He turned and walked back towards the garage just as Kesha was coming out the door.

"I found some keys on the table," Kesha said showing them to Doe, "but I don't know what they go to."

Doe looked at the keys then at the vehicles in the driveway. He grabbed a set from her and hit the panic button and a Toyota SUV's horn started going off. He shut it off then walked over and opened the doors.

Yetta and Nick came out the house as Doe was starting the truck. They all got in and took a deep breath before pulling to the end of the driveway. Doe pulled out his phone to call Gripp when Kesha got his attention.

"Doe," Kesha said looking at his face, where's Tony?"

James looked back and saw Black getting closer, so he pushed the pedal some more then got off on an exit. He made a quick right then a left into a parking garage and stopped at an entrance. They both jumped out and went into a building. Big Ben saw an elevator and walked over and hit the button. The door opened just as he heard tires rubbing.

Black hit the corner trying his best to keep up with the car but lost them when they took the exit.

"Where the fuck did they go," Gripp asked looking around, "it's like they vanished?"

"Naw," Black said pointing, "they went in that parking garage over there."

"What makes you think that," Gripp asked, "out of all these places."

"Because that's what I would've done, Black said turning into the garage, let's find out." He hit the corner and saw the car parked in front of an entrance as he pulled in the empty space next to a truck. After turning off the car he shifted to look at Fresh's body in the backseat and grabbed a gun then him and Gripp got out and headed for the building.

Gripp's phone rang as they were entering the building with a text from Doe saying, "got em". He smiled and put his phone back in his pocket. "They got the girls," Gripp said to Black, "now how the fuck we gonna find these niggas?"

"Honestly I don't know, Black said looking at the elevator, it's ten floors in this building and we don't know what's waiting for us up there."

"You right, fuck it, let's go." Gripp started walking back to the car.

"Why not?" Black said following him, "Let's enjoy today's victory."

They got back in the car and drove out of the parking lot. Black stopped at a gas station close to the highway to fill up and grab a snack. Gripp pulled out his phone and sent his location to Doe before he went into the store.

Doe sat in the driver's seat looking at Kesha not knowing how to answer her question without releasing pain behind it. He turned and looked at Yetta sitting under Nick then back at Kesha. She asked again

"Doe," Kesha said pushing his arm, "you not gonna answer me?"

"Kesha," Doe said looking down, "I really don't know..."

His phone interrupted him before he could finish his sentence. He looked at it and saw it was Pain calling so he handed the phone to Kesha. She smiled thinking it was Tony then laughed when she saw it was Pain.

"It would be him," Kesha said laughing, always interrupting shit."

"Well, I'm sure he wants a progress report," Nick said from the back seat, "you are his baby sister."

"Hello," Kesha said answering the phone, "what you want?"

"Who the hell is this," Pain said looking at his phone, "and where the fuck is Doe?"

"You need to see someone about that anger," Kesha laughed. "Or your ass gonna pop a vein or something."

"Oh my God," Pain said softly, "baby sis?"

"Yes, big brother," Kesha said wiping a tear, "it's me. I'm in the car with Doe, Nick, and Yetta. We're safe."

"My niggas," Pain chanted, "I'm so fucking glad they found ya'll and I hope they got his ass!"

"Hold on, Kesha said, I will let you ask Doe about that. I love you, Pain."

"I love you too, baby sis," Pain said holding tears, "see you soon."

"What up," Doe said when Kesha gave him the phone, "how are things looking in the city?"

"Quiet now," Pain replied, "but them two bitches kidnapped Nine ass."

"Word," Doe said sitting up, "is he good?"

"Yeah, he straight," Pain said, "the Baker Boys saved his ass."

The Bakers," Doe said sitting back, "hell I figured they would've left after the funeral the other day."

"Naw," Pain said, "they stuck around to give us a hand if we needed it and I'm glad they were in the right place at the right time."

"I can dig that," Doe said, "do me a favor and let everyone know we got em so my phone won't be blowing up during this long ass drive."

"Already but what's up with that nigga Ben," Pain asked, "I hope you made him suffer for what he did to Mastarpiece."

"That nigga got away from me bro," Doe answered, but I honestly think Black on his ass."

"Black showed up to the party?" Pain asked laughing, "I know he blew some shit up."

"Naw," Doe said laughing, "but we did kill a lot of niggas."

"Hell yeah," Pain said, "so did you tell them about Tony because if I know my sister she wondering where the fuck he at."

"You know I'm glad you brought that up bro," Doe said putting the truck in drive, "cause now you can tell them." He handed the phone back to Kesha as he drove away from the house. She put it on speaker phone before she spoke.

"Pain," Kesha said, "where is Tony and why isn't his ass here with Doe?"

"Kesha," Pain started, "Tony got shot trying to save ya'll that day. He still at the hospital."

"What are you saying Pain," Yetta yelled sitting up, what's going on with my brother?"

"He's fucked up right now," Pain replied, "and it's not looking good but you know Tony a fighter and will be fine once he sees you and Kesha are safe."

Nick looked at Doe through the rearview mirror and saw him shake his head, so he just sat back and kept quiet knowing they gonna expect Tony to be breathing when they get there. It was gonna be a long ass ride.

"Alright," Kesha said relieved, "we'll let you know when we're headed back." She hung up the phone and handed it back to Doe before putting on her seat belt. He dialed Gripp but didn't get an answer, so he pulled over at 7-11.

He was in the store getting a drink when a text came through from Gripp with a location. After putting it in his GPS, he paid for the drinks and gas and walked out to the car.

By the time he made it to the car, Nick was already pumping so he handed drinks to the girls and started to walk to the driver's side when Nick got his attention. "Aye Doe," he said pointing, "look who limping across the parking lot."

Doe looked over to see Howard as he made his way over to the store. "You have got to be shitting me," he said laughing, "shit I would've took one of them damn cars hell fuck that walking shit."

"Right," Nick said as he put the pump back, "that nigga probably took off limping as soon as we were out of sight."

"What the hell ya'll talking about," Kesha said opening the door, "and have either of you talked to my dad?"

"Yeah," Doe said, "he just texted me and we about to go meet up with him now. Then…" As Doe was talking Wesley pulled up to the store, got out and walked over to Howard. Kesha turned her head and instantly recognized Howard and Wesley. She reached in the car and grabbed the gun Doe gave her before he grabbed her arm.

"Girl, what the fuck you doing," Doe said holding her arm, "done lost your damn mind or something?"

"That nigga right there was one of the people in that van," Kesha said pointing at Wesley, "you see him?"

"Yeah, Doe said, I see him."

"You see how he walking and happy while my man laying in a fucking hospital fighting for his life?"

"Kesha," Doe said as he let her go, "now ain't the time for this."

Kesha smiled as she touched his face before cocking her gun.

"Oh it's time," she said, "past time."

She turned and aimed her gun at Wesley then fired off a shot hitting him in the shoulder. When he fell to the ground Howard pulled him to the side of the store. Kesha started walking towards them when Bret and Tom jumped out of the car.

"Fuck Kesha!" Nick said as he saw the guns coming out of the car, "told your ass to wait!"

Doe popped the trunk as he walked to the back of the SUV. He pulled out two shotguns and closed the trunk. Kesha just kept walking towards her target not worried about anything else. Doe tossed one of the shotguns to Nick then cocked his own. He aimed at the car and blasted hitting Tom as he made it to the back of the car. Bret fell to the ground and pulled out his gun.

"Stay here, Nick," Doe said walking, "and make sure nothing happens to Yetta."

He got low and fired another shot at the car. He looked and could see someone crawling under the car, so he shot again hitting the back of it. He heard Nick cock his gun as he turned and looked at Kesha. She was standing on top of Wesley, but Howard had a gun on her.

She looked into Howard's eyes as she held her gun to Wesley's head. Smelling the fear bleed from his pores, she pulled the trigger spilling his brains all over the parking lot. She continued looking at Howard before she turned around and walked back to the car. Doe turned to see Bret running down the street, so he headed to the car as well.

Kesha handed Doe the gun before she got in the car and closed her door. Nick had his gun on Howard until Doe got his attention.

"Let's go bro," Doe said, "we gotta meet Gripp."

"You sure you don't want me to blast this bitch," Nick said gripping the gun, "he already in my sights."

"Mane do what you gotta do," Doe said laughing, "I don't give a fuck about that nigga."

Nick pulled the trigger as soon as he said the words. Howard hit the glass of the store as his body fell to the ground. Nick and Doe put the guns in the trunk before they got in and headed to meet Gripp.

By the time Gripp came out of the store Black had already stolen another car and was waiting in a parking space by the door. He laughed as he walked over and got in. "Why did you switch cars, Gripp said closing his door, and where is Fresh?"

"I left his body in the other car, Black said, he don't need to take this ride and I will call Vance when we on the road."

Doe pulled into the parking lot beside them as Black was finishing his statement then let the window down. "Yadadi," Doe said when Gripp let his window down, "look who we got."

"Hey baby girl," Gripp said seeing Kesha in the front seat, "I'm so glad you ok and where's Yetta?"

"She in the backseat with Nick," Doe said letting the window down, "we gotta get the fuck out of here though cause Kesha just turned up at the gas station and them boys probably looking."

"For real Kesha," Gripp said laughing, "that's how you feel?"

She sat up and looked at him. "With my man laying in a hospital that's exactly how I feel."

"Aye," Doe said before Gripp had a chance to speak, "let's talk about all this at home." He put the truck in reverse, backed out, then pulled away from the gas station with Black following behind.

"Come on," Big Ben said as they made their way through the building, "I see an exit over there." He and James went out the door to the street and looked around but didn't see anyone, so they started walking.

"We need a car," James said getting tired, "I'm not trying to walk all day and night."

"I know," Big Ben replied, and we will deal with that later but right now we gotta get out of sight."

They continued to walk until they reached a hotel.

"Look," Big Ben said pointing at a valet, "you go distract him and I will steal some keys."

"What if he sees you," James asked, 'what you want me to do?"

"Figure it the fuck out," Big Ben said, "asking dumb ass questions."

James walked across the street and stood at the valet table looking at the guy hanging keys. He walked behind him and tapped his shoulder. When he turned around James punched him in the jaw knocking him out instantly. He reached into the box and grabbed a set of keys then walked back over to Big Ben smiling.

"Let's go," James said waving the keys, "the parking lot is over here.

"Idiot," Big Ben said laughing, "you definitely gonna get us caught doing stupid shit like that."

"Whatever," James said. They made it to the parking lot before he hit the button and the lights on a GMC Yukon came on. They walked over and got in and James started the truck and pulled out of the parking lot.

"So, where we headed," James asked pulling up his GPS, "I need to know which way to go."

"Head towards Killa City," Big Ben replied, "I ain't done with them mutha fuckers yet plus I still got one more trick up my sleeve."

"You just won't take the L," James said looking at him, "look at how many people we already lost."

"What's your point?" Big Ben asked.

"It's already gonna take us time and money to rebuild Houston," James started, "on top of trying to get Memphis back."

"So, what," Big Ben said, "I just do nothing and let them set up shop in my shit? Naw, I ain't going for that shit."

"Boss," James said, "listen to reason."

"How about you listen to me," Big Ben said, "and drive this fucking truck where I fucking said."

"Alright," James said, "but I got a bad feeling about this."

James put the city in his GPS and headed towards the highway. Big Ben let his seat back so he could get comfortable before he closed his eyes. James turned the radio to a soft volume and glanced over as Big Ben fell asleep right before he got on the highway.

They made it back to Killa City late in the evening. Doe got off the highway and headed towards Ma Williams house knowing that's where everyone was gonna be. He texted Gripp and let him know the destination.

Gripp looked at his phone and saw Doe's text. He showed it to Black then texted Bee to let her know they were back in town and headed to Ma William's house.

He sat the phone back on his lap and watched out the window as they drove through the streets of Killa City.

Yetta woke up as they were pulling into Ma William's driveway and pulling into the garage. She looked and saw Kesha was still sleeping before she sat all the way up.

"Why are we at my mom's?" Yetta said wiping her eyes, "instead of at the hospital with my brother?"

"I don't know Yetta," Doe said putting the truck in park, "this is where I was told to go."

"Kesha," Yetta said shaking her, "wake up cause something ain't right."

Kesha opened her eyes and sat up in her seat. She looked around seeing they weren't at the hospital. Doe touched her shoulder as she looked around the car. "What the fuck happened Doe," Kesha asked, "why are we here?"

"Come on," Gripp said when he opened Kesha's door, "Ma Williams waiting for us inside."

She turned around and looked at his face but couldn't tell what type of emotion he was feeling. He grabbed her hand helping her out of the car as Doe and Nick opened their doors. Black walked up and opened the door for Yetta.

Gripp looked up and saw Richard and Alex walking toward them, so he walked over to shake their hands. "What's up fellas, it's been quiet for yall?"

"Yeah, Alex responded, not too many issues while you were gone."

"What about Memphis," Gripp asked thinking about business, "our people in place?"

"They are definitely in place," Richard said laughing, "easiest takeover we ever had."

"That's what I like to hear," Gripp said tapping Richard, "any casualties?"

"Not a one boss," Richard answered, "like I said, the easiest."

"Ma Williams waiting for ya'll in the den," Alex said looking as Kesha walked up behind Gripp, "I'll hold

140

the door open for you." He turned and walked over to the door leading inside the house and held it open until everyone was in the house. He closed the door and went to sit at the kitchen table with Richard. Faba came in and shook Gripp's hand before he hugged the girls.

"It's truly good to see you both," Faba said, I'm glad you're safe and I'm truly sorry about Mastarpiece by the way."

"You and me both," Kesha said hugging him, "where is Ma Williams?"

"She's in the den," Faba said pointing, "come on and I'll take ya'll in."

Faba led the way as they walked through the house and headed to the den. When he opened the door, Ma Williams was sitting on a couch staring off into space. Gripp looked at her then back at Faba. He shrugged his shoulders and moved so Yetta and Kesha could go in.

Yetta ran to her mother and instantly wrapped her arms around her as Kesha came up and sat beside her. She looked at Ma Williams' face for a second before she spoke.

"Ma Williams," Kesha said grabbing her hand, "why are you here and not at the hospital?" Ma Williams turned and looked at Gripp just as Pain walked into the room.

"I'm home," Ma Williams started, "because I need to make some arrangements."

"What type of arrangements," Kesha asked, "he has insurance if it's money."

Pain walked up and touched Kesha's shoulder then she turned and looked up at him. "Tony's dead," Kesha said with tears in her eyes, "isn't he?"

"I'm sorry I lied to you sis," Pain said wiping her face, "but I didn't wanna tell yall over the phone."

"So, what happen, Yetta asked loudly, "how the fuck is my brother dead?"

"Calm down Yetta," Nick said trying to grab her, "no need to scream."

"No need to scream?" Yetta said getting up off the couch, "I lost my man, my brother and my best friend in a week's time!"

"I understand but…" Nick started.

"But nothing," Yetta said walking towards the door, "don't tell me to fucking calm down right now!" She walked out and slammed the door behind her. Nick started to chase her, but Ma Williams had Faba stop him before he made it to the door as she turned back to Kesha and held her hand.

"Kesha," she said, "Tony lost a lot of blood, and his injuries were more severe than any of us thought. Dr. McFadden did everything she could possibly do to save him, but he died yesterday."

"Yesterday," Kesha said crying, "why wouldn't any of you tell me that?"

"Because I told them not to," Ma Williams said taking the blame, "Tony was my son and I wanted you to hear it from me."

"I understand," Kesha said, "so where is Tony's body?"

"He is still at the morgue," Ma Williams replied, "we will go see him in the morning."

"Ok," Kesha said getting up, "I'm going to his room to shower then get some sleep."

Alright, dear," she said, "sleep well."

Kesha walked out and down the hallway towards his room but before she made it Yetta pulled her into the bathroom.

"I'm going to the hospital," Yetta said, "I have to see him for myself."

"Ma Williams said we were going in the morning, Kesha replied, "you really wanna upset her right now?"

"Girl I really don't care, Yetta said pulling out her keys, "wouldn't be the first time I pissed off my momma."

"Girl you crazy," Kesha said, "let's go."

"Says the one who shot up a gas station," Yetta said laughing, "you the crazy one."

They walked through the house and saw Alex and Richard still sitting in the kitchen, as they went out the patio door and to the driveway. Yetta unlocked the doors and they both got in as Kesha lit a blunt and they pulled out the driveway.

"So, I assume Ben is dead," Ma Williams said, "and his entire crew?"

"We got most of his people and set up in all his spots," Gripp replied, "but that bitch got away."

"Really, and you allowed that Black?" Ma Williams questioned.

"I didn't allow anything," Black said standing up, "he will get got once I locate his ass."

"I have no doubt," Ma Williams said laughing, "I'm just giving you shit."

"Oh, I know," Black said, "I'm just ready for a nap cause it's been a long ass day."

"You ain't lying about that," Doe said, "I'm gonna crash on the couch Ma cause I'm for damn sho tired of driving."

"Yes, everyone find a room or couch and get some rest. I will cook us all breakfast in the morning before we head to the funeral home."

"Aye," Doe said stopping everyone, "did they get Bam in the ground?"

"That they did," Pain answered, "I made sure of that."

"Yadadi," Doe said, "in the a.m."

"How much longer we got before we get there?" Big Ben asked waking up, "I'm getting hungry."

"We got about an hour and a half boss, James responded, but I can pull over if you wanna stop."

"Yeah, take the next exit," Big Ben said, "I gotta pee too."

144

"Alright," James said, "cool."

He took the exit and pulled over at a OnCue then parked by the gas pump. He handed Ben money for gas and drinks then watched as he walked into the store. Once he was in, James got out of the car and lit a cigarette waiting on the pump to start.

Detective White was sitting in his car playing scratch-off lottery when he saw Big Ben go into the store. He looked in his rearview mirror and saw James standing by the truck, so he picked up his radio and called for backup.

"Dispatch," he said, this is Detective White requesting backup at the OnCue off the Guthrie 77 exit to apprehend two fugitives."

He put down the radio then grabbed his sidearm before he got out of the car and walked over to James slowly watching his every move. Once he realized James didn't recognize him, he continued to walk until he was behind him. He grabbed him fast taking him to the ground and slapping cuffs on him. As he did that, Big Ben was coming out of the store and headed back to the car. When he was halfway there, he could hear the police cars getting closer, as he sped up thinking James was in the car.

He opened the door and got in but was shocked when James wasn't sitting inside. He turned to get out of the car but was met by the barrel of Detective White's gun.

"Don't be stupid," White said to him, "cause you know I will shoot the shit out of you."

"Fuck," Big Ben said dropping his hands, "ain't this bout a bitch."

Other officers were pulling in surrounding the gas pumps. Detective White talked to his captain while the others put James and Ben into squad cars. They all drove away as he took out his phone and sent a text and walked back to his car.

The next morning Gripp woke up to the kids and Bee sitting at the end of the bed. He sat up and kissed her before he grabbed his phone and read a text from White, he smiled putting his phone on the nightstand.

"Go ahead and take the kids downstairs," Gripp said getting up, "I will be down there in a few."

"Ok baby," Bee said, "did Kesha stay here last night too cause I didn't see her in Tony's room when I got here."

"She was probably in the shower," Gripp said putting on a shirt, "she was pretty tired."

"Hmm," Bee said walking out the door, "I guess."

Gripp went to the bathroom and brushed his teeth. He put on clothes before walking out of the room and downstairs. The whole crew was at the table once he made it to the kitchen. He looked around and didn't see Kesha or Yetta, so he pulled out his phone and dialed her but got voicemail. Ma Williams came out of the kitchen with maids following carrying plates full of food.

"Aye," Gripp said getting everyone's attention, where are the girls at?"

"They not still upstairs in their rooms," Pain said getting up, "I didn't see them leave."

"I didn't see them when I came down," Gripp responded, "and Bee say they wasn't there when she got here."

"That means they were gone before we laid down," Doe said, "cause no one walked by me but Bee and the kids."

"Ya'll don't think Ben got them again," Nine Milli asked, "do you?"

"Yeah, that's not possible," Gripp said laughing, "I got a text message from White saying he arrested Ben this morning."

"How the fuck White arrest him," Pain asked, "the nigga came straight here?"

"I guess so," Gripp said, "but at least we know he ain't got them this time."

"Then where the fuck they at," Skanes asked, "cause I'm hungry and ready to eat."

"They at the hospital," Faba said walking in the room, "left in Yetta's car last night. I had Alex and Richard follow them."

"Hard-headed ass girls," Ma Williams said shaking her head, "need to learn to listen."

Everyone laughed as she started passing the food around. Nick just stood looking out the window until one of the maids brought over a plate. He took it then sat beside Pain. Once most were done eating Ma Williams got up and walked over to the window then turned around so everyone could see her.

"Now that everyone is full and ready this morning it's time to get back to work,"'Ma Williams explained, "and let everyone know we are still standing."

"Ma, they know we standing," Pain said interrupting her, "hell we never fell."

"Someone came in our camp and took your sister as we tried to bury our soldier," Ma Williams said, "and that someone is still alive."

"You know what Ma," Pain said, "you got a fucking point but Gripp just said the bitch in jail so ain't shit I can do."

"See," Gripp said laughing, "that right there is why I'm the boss."

"Make sure the message is clear Gripp," Ma Williams said, "and I do mean crystal clear."

"I got you Ma Williams," Gripp said getting up, "he gonna for damn sure feel all the pain we feeling right now."

"Then it's official," Nine Milli said, "let's get up out of here and hit these streets."

Everyone started leaving the dining room and headed to the driveway. Gripp pulled out his phone and sent a text message as everyone started pulling out. He put his phone in his pocket and went to sit on the porch with Ma Williams.

"I've put things in motion," Gripp said sitting down, "should be done by the end of the day."

"You know Cain Locc is not gonna kill Big Ben," Ma Williams said looking at Gripp, "they have history."

"Cain ain't gotta do shit," Gripp said, "got someone else for that."

As Gripp finished his sentence, Yetta's car pulled in the driveway. She parked beside Gripp and her and Kesha got out and walked over to the porch. Kesha sat beside Gripp and Yetta sat on Ma Williams lap and laid her head on her shoulder. They sat in silence for a while before Kesha spoke.

"Can we go to the fields Dad?" Kesha said looking at Gripp, "I need nature to take this pain away."

"I take it you saw Tony in the morgue?" Ma Williams asked.

"Yes, we saw him," Kesha said softly, "still can't believe that he's gone plus I didn't even get to say goodbye."

Kesha started crying as Gripp grabbed a tissue from the table and handed it to her. He stood up and grabbed her and Yetta's hands and led them to his car. Ma Williams got up as they were getting in and motioned for Alex to get the car. Richard came and helped her off the porch before opening her door. Gripp lead the way headed to the fields.

The cell doors opened for lunch as Cain was waking up. He got out the bed and walked over to see if the guards were coming then turned to wake up Jermaine. Jermaine looked at Cain for a minute before he jumped down. Cain walked over and grabbed his cell phone and noticed he had a text.

Big Ben in there. No need to come out. CC

"Well, I'll be damned," Cain said pulling out a shank, "I guess you get to earn your stripes today my boy."

"What you mean," Jermaine said putting on a shirt, "what stripes I need to earn in here."

"Oh, you still think you here by chance," Cain said laughing, "naw player you may wanna hit your people and get the assignment."

"Bro, you tripping, what people you talking about?" Jermaine laughed nervously.

Cain dialed a number then threw the phone to Jermaine. He looked but didn't recognize it. When he put it to his ear, he heard a woman's voice and instantly recognized it.

"Sunee," Jermaine said surprised, "what the fuck is going on?"

"Big Ben just arrived there," Sunee said, "it's your job to kill him."

"Kill him," Jermaine said nervously, "why in the fuck would I do some stupid shit like that?"

"Nigga cause you ain't got a fucking choice," Sunee said, "contract is out and you been assigned so don't fucking get caught."

She hung up and left Jermaine looking at the phone. He turned and looked at Cain as he walked over smiling. He handed him a shank.

"Make it as painful as possible," Cain said, "so that bitch will hurt till his last breath."

"Why the fuck this shit on me," Jermaine said standing up, "they beef ain't got shit to do with me."

"Listen Jermaine," Cain said walking toward him, "this nigga killed Tony and MaStarPeace so he will die but why they chose you, I don't know."

"Wait," Jermaine said sitting down, "MaStarPeace is dead?"

"Yeah," Cain said, "he shot her in the head a few days ago."

"So, who made this call?" Jermaine asked, "cause I know it's a bounty out."

"Does it really fucking matter," Cain asked walking out the cell, "just get it done." Jermaine looked at Cain as he walked out the cell when a guard walked by, so he followed him as they headed towards the chow hall. He got in behind Cain as they waited on the chow line to move. They grabbed the trays and sat at the neighborhood table.

As Cain started eating Big Ben walked in with James behind him. Cain tapped Jermaine and he turned around just as they were getting in line for their chow.

"Aye Telly Cuz," Jermaine said looking around, "I need you to pop this shit off."

Telly looked around to see where the guards were before he stood up out of his seat. He looked at Cain and seen him point at James, so he slowly walked over and stood behind him in the line. He pushed James into Ben then started laughing loud as the whole room got silent.

"You lost your mind or something," James said looking at Telly, "you know who the fuck I am?"

"I know exactly who you are," Telly said laughing, "fucking dick sucker." He swung and punched James in the face then pushed him out the way so he could get to Ben. He grabbed his shirt before reaching back to punch him, but James grabbed him and threw him against a table.

Jermaine got up and was about to walk up on Ben when Cain stopped him. "Hold on Jermaine," Cain said grabbing his shoulder, the jakes coming."

"Fuck," Jermaine said sitting down, "can't do shit now."

"Just chill buddy," Cain said, "all part of the plan."

"What?" Jermaine asked but Cain didn't respond.

The guards ran over and grabbed Ben and James dragging them out as the others grabbed Telly. Once it was clear everyone started leaving the chow hall. Cain and Jermaine went in the cell and watched as fellow inmates did the same. Jermaine was sitting on the bed when Trap walked in the cell.

"We ready my nigga," Trap said to Cain, "everything in motion."

"Already cuz," Cain said, "good looking out. Let's go, Jermaine."

They got up and walked out the cell to the end of the block where a guard was waiting for them. He opened up a gate and told them to follow as he led them through the jail. He opened another gate and walked into Ben standing in one room and James in the other.

"You got 20 minutes," the guard said as he walked out, good luck."

"Get on your knees bitch," Jermaine said to Ben, "and I'm only gonna ask you once."

"Get on my knees?" Ben said laughing, "Nigga, fuck you."

Trap walked behind Ben and hit him making him fall to the ground. Big Ben spit on the floor before he looked at Trap.

"Both of you some bitches" Big Ben said trying to get up, "plus my momma hit harder than you. Trap punched him in the face pouring blood from his mouth. Big Ben fell back hitting the wall as Jermaine walked over and grabbed his face pushing the blade deep slicing a smile in Ben's neck. His body fell to the ground in a pool of blood. Jermaine looked up at Cain as he stared at Ben's body.

"Nigga you good," Jermaine asked Cain, "you zoned out or something?"

"I'm good lil nigga," Cain responded, "but you was supposed to find out where they bag was at."

"Oh, I still got one bitch to go," Jermaine said looking at James, "I'll find out."

"Aight," Cain said, "I'm in the pod."

Cain walked off headed towards A pod. He sat at a table watching movies waiting on the time to pass. He made a cross for Ben before getting up and walking to his cell. He made a soup before picking up his phone then sitting on the bed. As he was texting Gripp, Jermaine walked in the cell and took off his shirt. He threw it on the floor then jumped in his bunk without a word.

"Aye lil nigga," Cain said, "everything good"?

"Yeah," he responded, "we good. I'm going to sleep."

Cain laid on his bunk and closed his eyes

Gripp pulled to the gate and put the car in park. He got out and opened the gate and checked the mailbox before he got back in and drove down the mile long driveway. They parked in front of the stables and got out the car. Yetta walked over to the doors and was about to open them when Alex came from behind her and opened them first. She walked in and sat beside a horse as Gripp and Kesha went to the fields full of sunflowers. Kesha picked one up from the ground as they continued to walk.

Once they made it to the table Kesha said a prayer for Tony and MaStarPeace before she sat down beside Gripp.

They sat there till nightfall. The sound of Gripp's phone broke away their peace. He looked at the text and smiled hard.

"What is it dad," Kesha said looking at him, "what happened now?"

"Big Ben is no longer with us," Gripp said, "and they know where the stash is hidden."

"Seriously," Kesha said surprised, "but I thought Uncle Cain wasn't good with killing him?"

"He was ok with killing him," Gripp said getting up, "just wasn't gonna be the one to do it."

"We leaving?" Kesha asked, "I'm not ready to go. The sunflowers are peaceful."

"I have to go handle something," Gripp said kissing her forehead, "you can ride back with Ma Williams. I'm sure they all still in the house."

"Ok dad," Kesha said giving him a hug, "I love you."

"I love you too." Gripp said walking off. He passed Yetta as she made her way through the field. He hugged her but kept on going until he reached his car. He texted Ma Williams "done" before he pulled off and drove away.

"Thomas, the guard yelled, "bunk and junk."

"What the fuck is that nigga talking about?" Jermaine asked sitting up, "The fuck is bunk and junk?"

"Get your shit nigga," Cain said from under the blanket, "you getting the fuck out of here."

Jermaine grabbed his shit then nodded at Cain as the guard led him to processing. He changed clothes, signed paperwork then walked out the jail. He stopped mid step at the sight of Gripp standing by his car. He walked down the stairs and stood in front of him.

"You didn't tell me I was gonna be labeled a snitch," Jermaine said to Gripp, "niggas almost got at me."

"Them niggas wasn't gonna do shit," Gripp said laughing, "and you ain't got no damn charges. I already took care of that."

"Appreciate it, Gripp," Jermaine said shaking his hand, "I cut that nigga deep just like you asked."

"Already," Gripp said getting in the car, "let's go get something to eat." They hopped in the Chevy, turned on the music, and banged through the streets of Killa City.

One week later…

Ma Williams was sitting at the table watching the kids play video games as she waited on Black to finish the food. The park was packed full of people. Everyone came out for the balloon release and looked to be having fun on this hot ass day.

Faba was filling up the water balloons as the neighborhood kids stood in line ready to get wet. Once the bucket was filled he picked it up and carried it to the table.

The kids quickly attacked the bucket grabbing ballons and running through the park. Kesha and Yetta laughed as the watched the kids chase Faba and Alex throwing balloons as they walked around picking sunflowers.

Nick walked up and hugged Ma Williams as he looked at the crew playing dominoes. He leaned down and whispered something to her and she laughed. She pulled out her phone and texted Richard.

"Bring out 2 pairs of gloves."

She put her phone back down then looked over at the kids as Richard walked up with a box. He sat it down then stood beside her as she opened it and handed the gloves to Nick.

"You sure you wanna do this," Ma Williams asked sitting up, "cause it's not that big of a deal."

"Now Ma Williams," Nick said laughing, "you know I gotta get this bread."

"Well good luck," she said looking a him, " I hope you can take a punch."

Nick laughed again as he made his way to the Domino table. He stopped behind Tim and starred at Marcus before he dropped the bag on the table.

"You ready to do this shit?" Nick said putting on gloves, "Ma Williams said we gotta wear these."

"Oh you dead ass serious," Doe said getting up, I'm gonna beat the shit out of you."

"All that noise don't mean shit, Nick said throwing him the gloves, put that shit on and let's get it popping."

"You really wanna take this knock out cuz," Doe said taking the gloves, "I like free money."

Doe put on the gloves as they walked to the ring inside the barn Gripp trained in as a kid. They were getting ready to square up when Kesha and Yetta walked in the barn.

"Are yall seriously about to fight like some kids," Kesha said looking at Doe, "cause you know Tony wouldn't have this shit."

"Girl please," Nine Milli said handing her some money, "that nigga would say I got 50 bands on Doe."

"You right," Kesha said laughing, "well let's see a battle."

"That's what I'm talking about sis," Pain said laughing, "what about you Yetta?"

"All I got is this baby in my stomach," Yetta said rubbing her belly, "looks like Bam lives forever."

Everyone stood still at her comment. She turned as Ma Williams was walking up to her then they hugged with tears in they eyes.

"Enough with all that cry baby shit, Gripp said looking in the ring, "we can cry about that later."

"Really Gripp," Bee asked, like you don't have a tear in your eye?"

"Fuck that," Gripp said laughing, knock em out Doe."

"Yadadi!" Doe said looking at Nick. "Square up Nigga."

They danced around the ring until Doe swung first hitting Nick in the jaw but missed his second punch as Nick ducked and swung hitting Doe in the side.

"Damnnn", Pain said pulling out money, "I got 50 on Doe, who taking it?"

"Shiddddd me," Faba said counting, on Nick.

They were in the ring swinging connecting and missing punches till he hit the floor. Everyone stood up looking as he laid there breathing hard.

"You got knocked the fuck out!" Nine Milli said running in the ring.

"I told you got damnit, Richard said laughing, now give me my money!

The End

Crime Bluff Coming Soon

Made in the USA
Monee, IL
13 January 2023

23629562R00089